bro CODE

KENDALL RYAN

D1713794

Bro Code

Copyright © 2018 Kendall Ryan

Content Editing by Elaine York, Becca Mysoor, Angela Marshall Smith

Copyediting by Stephanie Atienza at Uplifting Designs

Proofreading by Virginia Tesi Carey

Cover Design by Uplifting Designs

This book is a work of fiction. Names, characters, places, and incidents are either the product of the author's imagination or are used fictitiously.

About the Book

There's pretty much only one rule when you're a guy.

Don't be a douche.

Turns out, the fastest way to break that rule is to fall for your best friend's sister.

Ava's brilliant, sharp-tongued, gorgeous, and five years younger than me.

She's the sexual equivalent of running with scissors. In a word, she's dangerous. And completely off-limits.

Falling for her could ruin everything.

Yet I can't seem to stop. Even when her company is threatened by a lawsuit and my promotion hinges on representing the opposing client—and winning.

I can't see a way out of this mess that doesn't end in a broken friendship, a broken heart, or a ruined career.

I may have broken the bro code when I fell for Ava. But do I have the balls to handle what comes next?

Chapter One

Barrett

IT'S BEEN A LONG time since I've been back to my hometown for a visit.

Nothing about the bar has changed since college, and when Nick comes around the table with a couple of beers the first sip tastes just like when I was twenty-one. Well, twenty with a fake ID, but this place is way too small for anyone to really care.

"Drink up, bro," Nick says, placing a pint of beer in front of me. We've been best friends since the second grade, and little has changed between us in all that time. "I'll get us something stronger once we're back at the house."

My heart almost stops before starting again. "I can't stay with your parents, dude. I'll just find another hotel." *One that isn't experiencing a water main burst.*

Nick shakes his head. "I already called my mom. She insisted that you stay, said she'd already changed the sheets in my old room."

Dammit. The beer I just swallowed sits uneasily in my stomach.

I certainly don't want to impose, and the nearest hotel is thirty miles away. But I can't let Nick know the real reason why I can't crash at his parents' house for the weekend. I can't stay there, and I definitely can't tell him why.

"How's work, man?" he asks, reaching for the basket of bar snacks and taking a big handful. "I'm surprised you had the time to make it down here."

I shrug. "Work is going well enough that they weren't worried about giving me the time off."

I'd been looking forward to the week back home ever since Nick invited me to his father's retirement party. And since Mr. Saunders was pretty much the only dad I knew growing up, I told him I wouldn't miss it. That and the chance to just relax and get away from the city was a welcome distraction. I haven't taken any time off in the past two years, and I called in a bunch of favors to be here this week, but it's worth it.

I'd expected to crash at my mom's place, but she waited until I was halfway through the drive here to tell me that the house was already full. I'd gone to the one hotel in town, only to find it closed for repairs brought on by water damage from a pipe bursting last week.

My mother has always done her best, but after she remarried, the kids that came after put me on the sidelines at home. It put a fire under my ass, enough to get an athletic scholarship for college and remold my dreams into going to law school. I passed the bar on my first try and hit the ground running, racking up hours at one of the biggest corporate law firms in Chicago. And now, at thirty, I have a new target—making partner, and eventually getting my name etched on the door.

"Still, I appreciate you coming down. Since my divorce, my parents have been on my back twenty-four seven," Nick grumbles. The split wasn't pretty. He'd only been married for three months when they filed divorce papers. Which was completely out of character for him. I still didn't have the full story, but something told me we'd get into all that once we were good and plastered this weekend. "Then this whole thing with Dad giving up the factory and..."

"How'd that end up working out?" Hearing Nick's dad had a heart attack was a shock. He wasn't that old, and had seemed in good health. Then he'd been forced into early retirement and the future of his factory hung in the balance.

After gulping down the rest of his beer, he shrugs. "My sister's taking over the place. I have no interest in learning to run some grease pit."

His sister. Every time Ava comes up, I have to keep a straight face. She's one of the only things about this town I ever missed, but Nick doesn't know. He'd deck me if he ever knew I looked her way, hell, that I even thought about her, and I wouldn't blame him.

Bro code is pretty clear about these things. Those unwritten rules are genetically coded into every male before birth. You don't hit on your best friend's sister. You definitely don't let your mind wander to what she looks like naked, and you sure as fuck don't let your dick go stiff at that thought. I force deep, measured breaths into my lungs.

"Sounds like she'll be busy." I keep my comment cool, almost off-hand, and wave down the bartender to get us another round. "Damn, it's barely seven and it seems like half the town's here getting hammered."

"Can't blame them." Nick casually glances at someone across the bar, and my gaze follows. "Jared Brown's over there with his third wife because it's their anniversary or something. Our old buddy Jacob has *four* kids now, if you can believe it."

How sad is your life that you take your wife to a random bar on a weeknight for your anniversary? I'd like to picture myself pulling out all the stops if I was in his position.

Nick continues, his tone turning sour, "The next eighteen years of his life are going to be spent saving up for college funds. I'm lucky I got out before that."

Honestly, Nick's parents are the only happily married couple I know. Has to be a generational thing because everyone else I run into from high school and college seem to be mired in misery, fighting with exes or trying to scrape the pieces back together before their kids notice. If I've learned anything, it's that settling down is a mistake. It's almost like no one really wants to commit, and they'll be hellbent on dragging you into a mess because neither side seems capable of being honest about what they actually want.

The single life gives me an advantage at work. Every weekend I watch as the other lawyers at the firm duck out early to try and squeeze in some family time amidst the ninety-hour work weeks. It's not something I have to worry about, and I know if I put my time in, it'll be rewarded. Sure, I spend more time at my desk going over assignments from the partners who are out to drinks with our clients than in my own bed, and my gym membership keeps slipping back further and further on my to-do list, but I'm so damn close to the top. Once I make partner, I've got the foundation for my future set in stone.

But all work and no play definitely makes a dull boy, as they say. Needing an outlet for all those hours spent with my eyes glued to my computer screen drafting contracts, I afford myself an occasional night of fun when I can get it. Admittedly, it's been a while since I did the horizontal mambo. There's just too much work, too many deadlines, and the goals I want to achieve, and I sure as hell won't let anyone take the top spot from me. There will be plenty of time to get laid after my promotion.

"Ah, shit." Nick's glaring at his phone, squinting at the screen in the bar's dim lighting. "Ava just got in, so my mom wants us both at the house already."

"Wait, she's going to be there, too?" The question slips out of my mouth before I think better of it, but Nick just laughs.

"Of course, she is. She just gave up her apartment and moved back in to be closer to the plant." Nick counts a couple of bills out of his wallet to pay his half of the tab; I drop my platinum card on top of them. "Let's get square and I'll drive us over."

I think the drinks we had have gone to my head. I'm looking forward to seeing Ava as much as I'm dreading sleeping under the same roof as her.

Fresh snow covers everything as we head out of the bar, little white flakes still falling across the parking lot. It's clean, untouched in a way that never lasts in the city, and for a moment I just stare at the blanket of pristine white that seems to almost shimmer in the moonlight. It's strange how you have to leave a place to find something you appreciate about it.

I chuckle to myself as Nick starts cursing and wiping the buildup off his windshield. He's never really appreciated the weather here.

"Remember when we used to have to shovel all this out of your driveway?" I ask.

"I remember *you* shoveling it because I told you it'd be great cardio," Nick jokes, grinning while getting into the driver's seat. "Then Mom came out and yelled at me because you were doing all the work alone."

"And who got paid double? I did." Smirking back at him, I ignore the middle finger Nick thrusts my way before he gets us on the road.

Constant traffic and people everywhere are what I'm used to in the city, but out here there's nothing but long roads and trees on either side, broken up by the occasional field or house. And huge expanses of starry sky. Someone with a plow hitched to his truck must have been working late, because the asphalt is scraped clean all the way to Nick's parents' house.

The place looks cheery with smoke floating from the chimney and lights glowing in the first-floor windows. I recognize his dad's old truck sitting in the driveway. Crazy that he's still driving that thing. A light dusting of snow covers it like it hasn't been moved in a while.

"Home sweet home." Nick parks behind the truck, then kills the engine so we can get out.

I ring the doorbell while Nick pockets his keys, and a second later the front swings open. Nick's mom greets me with a smile and the biggest hug I've ever gotten from anyone before doing the same to him, and I swear I see tears in her eyes as she claps her hands as she looks at me. The excitement of me staying here has put that joy on her face. I feel a little relieved that I'm not imposing.

"Barrett, I'm so glad you're staying with us." She glances back over her shoulder. "Ava, come say hi to everyone!"

Ava? Oh, fuck me. I haven't had enough time to mentally prepare for her being here, to silently chastise my dick to keep it in check, much less having her mom throw her in front of me as soon as I walk in the door. I'd just wanted a few minutes to ready myself for the reality.

Maybe she's changed. Hell, maybe she even went and got married and Nick didn't bother to say anything about it. I'm drumming up every excuse in the world to keep my blood from humming at the thought of Ava, because the last thing I need is my best friend roasting my balls like chestnuts because he realizes I'm into his sister. Really into her.

"Everyone?" Ava's voice carries to the doorway. "Who is every-"

Ava steps into view, and I take her in from head to toe in an instant. She was always a bit of a wallflower growing up, occupied with school instead of catching anyone's attention, but I remember the moment she blossomed.

It was a hot, sunny afternoon out at the lake one summer we came home from college. Ava was in high school then and Nick and I had tagged along with the group of teenagers, watching as they jumped from the rope swing, freefalling into what seemed like a forty-foot drop straight into the cold water below.

I watched Ava grab the rope, and let out a scream in mid-air as she jumped. After that, everything seemed to move in slow motion, because it was then that I noticed her hips, her breasts, and all that milky skin in her tiny two-piece swimsuit that did nothing for my hormones and everything for my fantasies. Bro code or not, I still had eyes, and a hundred adolescent dreams were just overwritten. God, she was beautiful then, but now she's grown into it, that sort of effortless look that...

Damn it. *Down, boy.*

I know better than this. At least, I'm supposed to. Ava's eyes lock on mine, surprise playing out across every inch of her expression. She must not have expected to see me—at least, not so soon. By reflex, I smile, and even under the dim glow of the lamp in the foyer, I'm pretty sure her cheeks turn pink.

"Hey, Ava. It's great to see you," I say, sidelining that sudden rush of lust into an attempt at good manners.

If this keeps up, I'm going to have to sleep in the snow to keep the lust filled heat flowing through me to an appropriate level.

"Uh, hello, Barrett." She takes a step back so Nick and I can come inside, and wipe our boots off on the rug.

"We're making some cookies in the kitchen. I remember your appetites from when you were growing up." Nick's mom smiles and then walks toward the kitchen. "Ava, let's go finish the dough."

"Right. Sure thing." Her answer is a little distant, her eyes still locked on me. "How's everything with you, Barrett?"

"Great." I don't want to brag, but it's the truth. "How about you?" It's been years since we really connected and suddenly I want to know everything about her. I want to know what makes a twenty-five-year-old woman give up everything to talk over a struggling factory in rural Indiana.

"Well, you know..." She bites her lip, and it distracts me until Nick taps my arm.

"Let's go upstairs, man. Come on," he says, and I nod, not wanting to give myself away. When I look back toward Ava, though, she's gone.

Shit.

No, that's a good thing. The more space we have between us, the better, and I can keep my focus elsewhere. With a deep breath, I pull my head together, and follow Nick upstairs and into his old room. Everything's neat and cozy, and it's crazy how being here immediately brings me back fifteen years. Everything about this small town feels like a time machine.

"You'll stay in here," he says, reaching up to tug open the knot of his tie, giving himself a little breathing room. "I'm going to crash down in the den since the flat screen's there. Not to mention a whole lot of booze."

I think his quickie marriage and even faster divorce fucked with him more than I've realized, but I nod. "I think I'm done drinking for the night." We'd only had a few beers, but the last thing I wanted to do was throw my self-control out the window when Ava would be sleeping one door over from me. "I might catch some early Zs so I'm not wiped out with everything we have going on tomorrow."

"You say that like my mom isn't going to be fawning all over you tomorrow, making sure you have everything you need, cooking you your favorite breakfast, hugging you every chance she gets." Nick grins.

I can't help but return his smile. Sometimes I think his mom likes me more than my own. "Your mom is pretty damn epic, if I do say so myself. But I'm just beat, it's been a long-time coming for me to just shut my brain down and relax, ya know."

"Sure thing, man, whatever you want," he continues. "I'm just glad you're here. Catch you in the morning."

"Thanks. I want to say hello to your dad, then I'll probably shower and hit the sack."

The image of Ava tangled in the sheets in the room next to me flickers across my brain again, and I hold back a sigh. Considering my deviant thoughts, it's probably going to be a very cold shower.

Chapter Two

Ava

My mom would say that plans are like cookies—no matter how closely you follow the recipe, something completely different can pop right out of the oven.

It's why she laughs when I spill an extra tablespoon of vanilla into the batter we're making, and I hold back a groan. There's no getting it out once it's in, and we're way too far along to start over. All I can hope now is that some miracle of chemistry will even things out once they're on the tray.

"You look so serious, sweetie," Mom chides, folding everything into the dough so it can be mixed and then rolled flat across the counter. "Relax. This weekend is going to be fun."

"Sorry, Mom." I wish that she wasn't always so perceptive. "I've just got a lot on my mind."

Not the baking. Baking is easy street next to Barrett.

He's the reason I wish my vibrator wasn't packed away with all my other belongings deep in the garage…and he shouldn't even be here. My brother could have told me he was bringing his best friend to the house for the weekend, but no, I get to relive a fifteen-year-old crush—in the flesh—because Nick doesn't know how to make a phone call.

Typical Nick.

Absence makes the heart grow fonder, and apparently it also turns the cool, older guy I dreamed about having my first kiss with into the best-looking man I've ever seen. Ever. I only caught a glimpse when he came in with Nick earlier, but it was enough to make my heart almost stop before I quickly darted into the other room.

That jaw, that *smile*, and he was so tall…

Barrett had always been taller than me, though. At fourteen, 'sexy' had barely entered into my vocabulary, but when all my friends were cooing over Hollywood heartthrobs and boy bands, I was looking at Barrett. He was the good guy, the guy you could trust, and he kept my brother out of trouble more than once. I'd catch glimpses here and there, but Barrett always seemed to be just out of reach—at least until I turned seventeen.

My birthday party that year had transformed into a nightmare after I'd gotten into a huge fight with my best friend and I wanted to be anywhere but in the house. The only place to go was the backyard, where I'd been crying my eyes out until a hand touched my shoulder. Barrett was the last person I expected to see when I turned around, concern written all over his face.

"Hey, Ava. You okay?"

I don't remember what I said back. Whatever my answer, it wasn't enough to convince him, and a second later, I was wrapped in the tightest hug of my life. He let me cry my eyes out against his chest until I had nothing left, and when I cursed out my friend for being such a pain, Barrett's laugh was a warm, deep rumble in his chest. When I was finally able to put myself back together, he walked me back inside where I made up with my friend.

We never talked about it again. I don't know if he thought my brother would give him shit for being sweet to me or what, but it lingered in my mind for months. Years now, I guess.

"Ava, honey, let's get this batch going." My mom's voice draws me back into the present, and so does the aluminum cookie cutter she's waving in my face.

When I lean over to check the recipe card, she shoos me away from it, pushing the cutter right into my hands. "You don't need to count how many you make per tray. Just shove them all on there."

Sue me for wanting them to bake evenly through. "Okay, Mom."

I press the little tree and star outlines into the dough over and over, cutting out dozens of cookies. Each one goes onto the tray, and my mom scrapes the excess together before rolling it flat again, which is just enough for two more cookies. Once they're arranged in a bunch of clean rows, I'm urged out of the kitchen.

"I'll call you back in when it's time to frost them," Mom says.

There's not much else to do but wait for the scent of fresh cookies to fill the house, so I slip down the stairs and into the den. My dad is exactly where I left him a few hours ago, watching the news on the couch, but now that the sun's set, the entire room is dark. He doesn't seem to have noticed, but I flip on a lamp anyway before sitting down next to him.

"What's the state of the world like, Dad?" I ask.

He mutters something under his breath, eyes still locked on the screen. "Same as always. Your mother run you out of the kitchen?"

"Yeah." I don't mind, though, and he knows it. "You shouldn't stay down here in the dark, you know. It'll kill your eyes."

"Not like I need them for much anymore."

The bitterness in my dad's voice is new, raw. After decades of building a business with his own two hands, a heart attack last fall suddenly put him out of commission. Every doctor said it was congenital, that only a life of hard work and eating well had kept severe heart problems from starting earlier, but that was almost worse in a way. If there had been something he could change, my dad would have immediately put his nose to the grindstone and fixed it. Instead, he had to retire.

Now I'm taking over where he left off. It would have been Nick's job but he loves living in the city, and being a store manager who gets to drink with the guys every night too much to stop and learn how to run a factory. When Dad asked, my brother said he'd just close the business and sell it off, locking the doors on the same place whose profits put him through college. Thinking about that conversation always puts a boulder in my stomach.

I refuse to shut down the factory. My dad has hundreds of employees, from janitors to engineers, and they all rely on the company staying open. Every business around it would buckle without those people keeping a steady paycheck. I've driven past enough towns that were left to turn to dust and blow off the map because someone didn't care enough to keep the heart of it alive.

"You know what the boys are up to?" Dad asks, squinting at the screen in front of him.

I reach over to the table next to the couch, grabbing the case for his glasses. He sighs, but takes them anyway. "Not really. Barrett walked in and then Nick dragged him off."

"Some things never change." Now that he can see, my dad looks at me instead of the television. "I'm glad you came home to start looking things over, Ava, but I wish you weren't by yourself. I'm so proud of you, but you deserve someone to share a life with."

Oh God, this again. "Dad..."

"You're twenty-five." He frowns, wrinkles pulling against old laugh lines. "You know, your mom and I were-"

"Twenty when you started dating. I know." It's the same story he brings up every time he sees me lately, and somehow, I feel just as guilty every time. He means well, of course, and I've never wanted to disappoint him. "I'm working on it, okay? But I've got to get everything with the factory stable first."

I don't think navigating the ins and outs of running the factory will be too bad, despite the learning curve. Even if I don't know anything about building new engines, I did go to school for business management. After graduating, I stuck almost exclusively to consulting work, but this could be the chance for a real career, something I can settle into for good. Then I can find Mr. Right and see about having a couple of kids before my mid-thirties start to loom on the horizon.

Which means dating again. Which means going on a date in the first place, instead of focusing on how I've been single so long. That's a rabbit hole I'm determined not to go down, unless I find myself in the mood for a good cry later.

"I'm not rushing you." Dad gives my shoulder a fond pat. "I just don't want you to be alone. You've got a lot to offer a man."

"I'll put that on a sign next time I go up for auction," I tease, and he chuckles before shaking his head.

"Ava! The cookies are ready!"

It's kind of amazing how my mom can make her voice carry through an entire house. There's a reason I never got away with anything as a teenager.

Dad gives me a little salute. "Duty calls."

I hustle back up the stairs to the kitchen, ready to be wrist-deep in frosting and sparkles until every cookie looks appropriately festive. Thankfully, I get a system down quickly, and once my mom's stretched clear wrap over the tray, I'm ready to wash my hands and relax with a glass of wine. That master plan is swiftly derailed by my mother stacking the dishes under the faucet and shooing me out of her way.

"Use another sink, honey." She's already turned away from me, looking in the cabinets for a washcloth. "I've got to wipe everything down before the dough sticks like glue."

Trudging up another flight of stairs to the bathroom, I nudge the door open with my elbow before stepping inside. The light is already on, and I have about a second to register why before the shower curtain slides back against the wall.

Barrett steps out from behind it, and my thoughts scramble in sixteen different directions at once. I've known those brilliant blue eyes for years, but not the way water looks clinging to his dark eyelashes, or dripping down his sculpted frame, the valleys and ridges of all that muscle, the sheer breadth of his shoulders. He towers over me, making it easy for my eyes to draw lower, tracking a single, clear drop from his chest down to his chiseled abs.

The lucky little drop falls into fine, dark hair, neatly trimmed around the thick base of—holy mother of mercy—the largest penis I have ever seen. My breath catches in my throat and I have the sudden urge to take a step back, and I would have, had I not been rooted in place so firmly. I wasn't sure my legs would ever work again.

Heat sparks under my skin and settles as a needy pulse between my thighs as I take in the impressive length of his shaft. Even soft, he's huge, and that thought is all it takes to imagine Barrett hard and so deep inside me, that powerful body pinning mine right to the wall. With all that muscle framing his hips, he could keep me there, taking me over and over until we were both totally exhausted...

Now he's not the only one who's dripping wet.

I've never been madder at myself before, remembering again how far away my vibrator is right now.

"Uh, Ava?" Barrett's very real voice snaps me out of my erotic fantasy. "Are you okay? I'll be out of here in a second if you need the bathroom."

I was staring at him. I've been staring at a naked Barrett Wilson, my brother's best friend, for a full minute, straight-up ogling like he was in a dirty magazine. What was I thinking? My first attempt at words come out as an intelligible whimper, and my face is heating up so fast I'm pretty sure something in my brain is about to short-circuit. No, scratch that; all of me is going to short-circuit.

My nipples pebble inside the cups of my bra, and my heart hammers dutifully behind my ribcage.

Making no move to cover himself, Barrett smiles, and somehow that makes everything ten times worse. "Ava? Can I help you?"

There's a hundred ways I want him to help me, and every single one involves having my clothes ripped off, his body on top of mine. Except I can't do any of that when I'm staring at him like a total fool, and this isn't supposed to be how my evening ends.

I don't have a plan. The only thing I can do is rush out of the bathroom, yanking the door shut behind me. It slams a bit loudly, but at least I can start to pull myself together with a barrier between me and Barrett's gorgeous body. Those sinfully perfect abs, his sharp jawline, that stunning face, and most of all, the baseball bat-sized appendage between his legs.

My evening was going to end with a relaxing glass of wine. The only thing I know right now is that there's not enough wine in this county to calm the fire Barrett has ignited inside me.

Chapter Three

Barrett

The door slams, and with it all the oxygen in the room seems to disappear.

Holy fuck.

Ava had barged in on me, and had gotten one hell of an eyeful. Watching her take in every inch with surprise lighting up those beautiful eyes—my cock twitched. Even with my prompting, she hadn't said a word before dashing out of the bathroom, but I swear before the door slammed shut behind her, that shock became something more—for just a split second. It had transformed into something hotter and a whole lot less innocent.

She wanted me.

I'm trying to convince myself that it isn't just my dick talking.

But the thought gets me so damn hard that before I can picture anything else, my cock strains up toward my stomach and demands attention. I glance back at the shower, wondering if I should burn through the rest of the hot water and rub one out or turn it to the right and let the cold wrangle my hard-on back into submission.

"I must have been seeing things," I say out loud, combing my hands through my wet hair. I've got to find a way to make those words true, because the alternative is off-limits.

I've known Ava for years, and she's never looked at me like that. With Nick and I hanging out together all the time, I must have seemed more like another brother than anything else. She'd never shown a hint of any interest when we were younger.

Closing my eyes, I try to knock that thought away. The problem is, my cock is happy to do the rest of the thinking for me, and if I don't get a handle on it, I'll be spending the rest of the night blue-balled and frustrated with the object of my fantasies mere feet away from me. Better to blow off steam now instead of trying to sneak a quick jerk off session later. I twist the lock on the door, something I should have done in the first place, and I place one hand against the tiled counter, while my right hand slips down to my shaft.

I could get it over with fast, vent the tension coiling through me with a dozen old and reliable images, but the only thing that comes to mind and sticks is Ava. Her wide, blue eyes filled with surprise, the tiny shudder that passed through her when she saw me.

I imagined how she'd touch me, unsure at first, using slow, tentative strokes as she learned my cock, then moving faster as she found some confidence in handling its size. The closer I got, the more she would tease, drawing out her touch until I couldn't take anymore, threatening to blow then and there. I roll my thumb over the sensitive tip, imagining the look on Ava's face as she dropped to her knees and—

"Goddamn it," I curse under my breath, but my hand doesn't stop.

She's off-limits. She absolutely has to be off-limits. I lean heavily against the counter to keep myself steady while pumping in firm strokes, trying to get my libido focused on any woman but her. But nothing is satisfying enough compared to the thought of her mouth on me— except for imagining pinning her down to my bed, her body wrapped around mine like a vise. I would give her everything she asked for, until I was sure I was the best she ever had. Hard or slow didn't matter, as long as I could see Ava's face the moment her orgasm hit and bliss overwhelmed her, milking me for all I was worth.

My breath quickens, muscles rippling in my forearm as I squeeze the base of my cock, ratcheting up the tension until pleasure blazes hot through my entire body, come spilling in thick spurts over my hand.

Holy shit.

I wash away the evidence in the sink, but the feeling doesn't fade until I finally deflate. Another passing thought of Ava almost makes me twitch, but for the moment I've got everything on lockdown.

"Behave," I mutter under my breath while turning off the water, "or Nick and I are going to end up in a fist fight in the middle of the goddamn snow."

After towel-drying my hair, I wrap the towel around my waist and go into Nick's old room, unzipping my overnight bag where it sits on the bed. I yank out a pair of sweatpants and a college football shirt to sleep in, running a thumb fondly over the fading logo. A cabinet in the corner of his rooms displays the trophies we won proudly. Mine are in a box somewhere in my mom's garage. At least I think they are. Unless she sold them at her last garage sale. I have a thousand memories of Nick's parents cheering us on, with Ava watching with her friends in the stadium.

Most of the time my mom couldn't make it. The school only gave me a handful of free tickets a year, and they usually weren't enough for her and my siblings. Getting a babysitter on her strict budget was out of the question. I handled it alright, though. I always knew that someone was rooting for me, even if she wasn't there. Nick's family has always had my back.

Which is why I have to quit thinking with my dick. I'm here for the Saunders family retirement party, not to get laid. If I can't keep a hold of myself for a long weekend, what kind of man am I, anyway?

A knock on the door stops that train of thought cold. "Yeah, come in."

When the latch clicks open, the last person I expect to see standing there is Ava. The faint blush on her cheeks I glimpsed in the bathroom is gone, but that doesn't mean I can stop thinking about what that warm color looked like. Her smile is a quick flash of teeth, cute as I remember from so long ago. If anything, it suits her more now, with a little crinkle at the side of her mouth like she's trying not to grin.

"Hey, Barrett. I just wanted to apologize for earlier." She sighs, her eyes not quite meeting mine. "I barged in on you without even knocking."

"It's no big deal. I'm in your house, not the other way around." I want to tell her exactly how much I didn't mind, how much her unexpected voyeurism inspired every moment of my jerk off session a few moments ago, but I know better. The logical part of my brain knows better, anyway. "You okay, though? You were kind of like a deer caught in the headlights."

What the fuck is that cheeky, challenging tone to my voice?

The heat returns to her face, a blush that she doesn't even bother to hide. "Yeah, well, you ended up being a lot...well...more than I was expecting." She clears her throat.

"I was, huh?" It's impossible not to tease Ava when she's playing coy. Literally impossible. "Sorry, I'll keep it in its cage next time."

"You're such an ass," she says, but chases the words with a laugh. I can't remember the last time I heard Ava laugh—it's been years. I missed that sound more than I realized, enough to make her want to do it over and over again.

Running a hand back through my hair, I give her an exaggerated, innocent look. "I didn't think my ass was the part of my anatomy in question."

A good-natured roll of her eyes has me grinning, and my shoulders relax by a few degrees. This can just be banter, just be fun without any screw-ups. We haven't talked in a long time, so maybe now is my chance to do that. Focus on the friendship, because sex certainly isn't on the table.

"You're alright though?" I ask again, needing to hear her say it, needing some reassurance that I didn't scar her for life or make her too uncomfortable to sleep right across the hall from me for the next four days.

"Yes, it's just. Okay, in all seriousness ... how do you walk around with that in your pants all day?" The determined look on her face is priceless.

"I strap it down to my leg with duct tape," I say in the most serious voice I can muster.

Her eyes widen. "Holy shit, seriously?"

Unable to hold in my laughter, I chuckle at her. "No, Ava. That was a joke."

Her cheeks are bright red again, and fuck, what is this perverse part of me that likes teasing her. Maybe because it feels a lot like flirting, something I've never allowed given our age difference.

She breaks into a laugh, her shoulders relaxing and we spend the next few minutes reminiscing about the football games she attended of mine and Nick's throughout high school and college, and it's crazy how at ease we are with each other. A few minutes of talking and we're both laughing, remembering some of the stupid shit her brother and I used to do. I guess some things never change.

"You're doing well?" I ask, genuinely wanting to know.

"I'm good," she says. Her eyes are just as blue as I remember. The rest of her, however? She's grown and filled out in ways I never imagined.

"You look good."

Fuck.

Why did I just say that?

She looks right at me then, and holding her gaze is harder than I expect. I don't want her to sense what's on my mind, to have any idea what I was just doing a few minutes ago while thinking about her. Even if by some miracle she felt the same way, Nick would flip and for good reason. He's been my best friend since we were six, and his whole family practically took me in. Paying that back by sleeping with his baby sister over a long family weekend would make me a complete asshole.

Besides, I'm leaving in a couple of days. It'd be one thing to be dating Ava and break the news to Nick at the right time, but I don't have time for a relationship. I barely have time to go to the gym or eat a dinner that's not at my desk. My life is in Chicago, and hers is going to be here in Indiana with the factory. I can't be two places at once while trying to make partner. I barely got enough coverage to slip away for the weekend, and the last thing I'm hunting for now is something serious. I turn and stretch my arms over my head, feigning a yawn. Otherwise, I'm about to do something really stupid. Like try to kiss her. Or show her my dick again.

"I guess I should be getting to bed. It's late." She turns to step through the door, but pauses one last time to say over her shoulder, "Sorry, again."

"It's okay. You'll just have to return the favor sometime." The words slip out of my mouth before I realize how they sound, and I've never been so glad to hear Ava giggle and close the door on me.

Damn, that was *way* too close to crossing the line. Teasing her is one thing, but actually flirting back is asking for trouble. That's not a game I can afford to play, much less win.

I turn off the lights before I can do something I'll really regret and sink down onto Nick's old bed. It used to be big enough for us to sit side by side and play games, but now my feet hang over the edge. I laugh to myself, moving the pillow back a couple inches so I can actually lie down the proper way.

Alone in the dark, my mind starts to wander, and I'm way too keyed up for sleep despite my excuses. Getting off just once in the bathroom wasn't enough to set my body at ease, not when simply talking to Ava has me this worked up all over again. Sure, I'd been looking forward to this visit but I hadn't thought there was anything in this state to really miss. I'd outgrown Indiana. Chicago looked like the perfect land of opportunity in my twenties and I couldn't get out of this little town fast enough to pursue my dreams.

Except she's still here, trespassing through my thoughts. I have to keep reminding myself she's off-limits; she loves her parents too much to leave, and with the factory passing into her hands, she's anchored to this place. It's simply one more reason in a laundry list of others as to why I can't have her, and why I shouldn't even be thinking about it. In a few days, we'll both be back to our own lives, and we'll forget about each other all over again.

At least, I sure as hell hope so.

Chapter Four

Ava

It has easily been almost ten years since I cracked the spine on my high school yearbook, but after seeing more of the star of my freshman fantasies than fifteen-year-old me ever dreamt up, I find myself wanting to wander down memory lane. Last night's dreams featured an alternate reality where I was allowed to touch and tease Barrett, watching his eyes darken with lust. Waking up to the reality that I had ogled his package for a solid minute somehow felt less magical and a hell of a lot more awkward.

But wanting to hold on to my fantasy a little longer, I roll out of bed and scan the bookshelf until my finger falls upon the familiar bright blue plastic binding of my sophomore year edition of the Harrison High yearbook. I settle back into bed, flipping past football photos and ghosts of prom dresses past until I land on the spread of the freshman class. There I was, one tiny rectangular picture in a line of portraits preserving memories of hairstyles that we'd all rather forget. Even in that tiny picture you can tell how skinny I was. My curves didn't really start showing up until after high school graduation, and by then, Barrett was already through his undergrad and in law school on the east coast.

I lock eyes with the teenage version of myself with stick-straight brown hair and a mouth full of braces, wondering if Barrett still sees me like this—his best friend's lanky, metal-mouthed little sister.

I sure don't think of him as just a hunky football player anymore, but then again, after last night I'm not certain I'll be thinking of him any other way than naked, dripping wet from the shower. Still, talking to him last night was fun and, shockingly, less awkward than I would've expected after the shower mishap. But this is my brother's best friend, and the rules, although not always spoken, are incredibly clear. Despite my lingering feelings for him, talking is as far as things can go.

I reach for my phone to check the time—it's later in the morning than I thought, and the longer I wait to claim the bathroom, the slimmer the odds of any hot water being left for me. I slide the yearbook back into its place on the bookshelf, then head off to the bathroom. I make a point of locking the bathroom door behind me. No repeats of last night with me on display instead.

I miss the privacy of the bathroom in my apartment, but since moving back home to take over the plant, one of the very few things that has remained the same is my shower routine. From the moment I step into the bathroom, it's all second nature. I turn the handle all the way to the right before shimmying my pajama pants off my hips, letting the steam inch over the corners of the mirror. Next comes the facemask, which I squeeze into my palm and smear across my cheeks and nose, my skin tightening pleasantly as the mask cements. With so much time spent stressing over Dad's health and the future of the company, the few moments where I get to take a deep breath and focus on myself are more valuable than ever. These moments are what keep me sane.

After my shower I pick out a cozy red sweater that hugs my frame in all the right places and swipe a thick coat of mascara over my lashes. There's no point in applying a full face of makeup, there's too much party prepping ahead of me. The whole house smells like eggs and bacon grease. Which I'm sure is the result of Mom's excitement of having a house full of 'kids' to cook for again, but when I walk into the kitchen, Nick is the one laying bacon in a pan. Mom and Dad must have already left for Dad's doctors' appointments.

"Good morning," I say, selecting an especially crispy piece of bacon from the plate that Nick has piled up.

"How'd you sleep?" he asks, sliding an egg off the skillet and onto a plate.

My face threatens to heat again at the memory of last night. "Not too bad. And thanks for cooking. This looks great."

Nick shrugs. "I can't take all the credit. I was totally prepared to eat cookies for breakfast. Barrett was the one who suggested something a bit heartier."

I turn around and, sure enough, there's Barrett, somehow making pouring coffee look like a sex act. I focus with laser-like intensity on the handle of the coffeepot to avoid letting my eyes wander up his forearms to his shoulders or worse - down to check if those sweatpants are showing off a second viewing of last night's performance.

"Want some?" he offers. I snap out of it to see that, unfortunately, he's gesturing at the coffeepot and nothing else. There's plenty I want from Barrett, but coffee has very little to do with it.

"You might want to take that to go," Nick says. "We were talking about heading out to pick up party stuff once we get these dishes done."

"How about you two go ahead and I'll take care of the dishes?" I offer. "Teamwork."

As if on cue, Nick's phone buzzes on the counter. He snatches it up and answers it with a sly grin.

"Hi Dana, I'm so glad you called back." He presses his phone against his chest to mute things on his end. "Would you guys mind covering party supply duty?" he asks.

Barrett smirks, but agrees with a nod and a slow sip of coffee. I remember Dana, one of Nick's high school flings. I haven't heard him mention her in years, but who am I to stand in the way of his romantic endeavors?

The phone goes back up to Nick's ear as he mouths an exaggerated "thank you" to the two of us before escaping up the stairs.

"Some streamers, a few balloons," Barrett says. "Nothing we can't handle, right?" He shoots me the sexiest smile and I clench everything.

"We can take Dad's truck," I suggest as I break Barrett's gaze. "Plenty of room in the back." I hesitate before adding "for the decorations."

I can't believe my luck. Me. With Barrett. Alone. I throw my half-eaten piece of bacon into the trash. Suddenly my stomach is too full of butterflies to make room for anything else. What was that pep talk that I gave myself about not going any further than talking?

"Well, we might as well head out now," Barrett says, downing his coffee and placing both of our empty plates into the dishwasher. "Do you want to grab a coffee to go?"

His concern for my caffeine intake is sweet. Either that or I'm totally losing my mind. "Good plan," I murmur, helping myself to one of my dad's stainless steel mugs.

I grab the keys to Dad's truck off the hook and toss them in Barrett's direction. "I'll navigate if you drive," I offer.

Somehow, putting me behind the wheel with Barrett riding shotgun sounds like a recipe for disaster. Add the snow and ice on the roads and I'm practically guaranteed to fishtail. How could I keep my eyes on the road when six inches to my right is the star of my teenage sex dreams? Who am I kidding, he was the star of last night's sex dreams, too.

Barrett grabs his trim, black coat off the back of a kitchen chair and I can hardly believe how handsome he looks in it. Suddenly, I completely regret packing my classic wool winter coat. It's two boxes over from my freaking vibrator. My puffy jacket may be practical for Indiana winters, but it's not doing me any favors in the sex appeal department. I skip the hat to keep from looking like a complete snowman and we're out the door.

The first half of the drive to the party store is relatively quiet aside from me providing the directions. But my thoughts run wild and it's hard to concentrate when I can almost feel his body heat radiating next to me.

I haven't run errands in my hometown since I'd moved back from my apartment a few towns over, but I still have my bearings for the place. It seems like Barrett, on the other hand, has completely wiped his memory of rural Indiana and replaced it with Chicago train schedules. At every red light, he rubs his hands together to give himself a little extra heat. Half of me is tempted to reach over and offer to help warm him up, but the smarter half of me forces my hands into the pockets of my coat. Hands to yourself, Ava.

"Sorry you're getting roped into all this party planning business," I finally say, my best attempt at small talk to pull me out of my fantasy.

"No worries, I'm happy to help."

Silence again.

Why am I totally coming up blank? There are plenty of questions I could ask. How is life in the city? How are things going at work? I'm frozen solid, and not just because of the cold. I'm afraid that if I open my mouth, I'll ask the only real question on my mind. Will you show me what you can do with that glorious cock? *Please*.

"How is it taking over your dad's business?"

Barrett with the save. I'm so grateful that he's broken the silence that I hardly mind that it's a question with an especially tricky answer.

"It's good, but not exactly stable," I admit. "The plant is pretty much breaking even at this point. Nick seems to think I'd be better off just selling the place since it's not making much money, but I care about all the workers so much. Dad has worked with some of them since I was a kid, and I just don't know what would happen to all of them if I were to sell. Plus, I like a challenge. It's exciting, you know? And having ownership in something—being the one to make the decisions, to call the shots. I love that aspect of it."

I'm rambling. I didn't realize how much I needed to talk about this. "What do you think?"

He's quiet for a second, thinking it over, so I turn my head to look out the window to avoid staring too long. I shouldn't have said so much. He probably thinks I'm crazy. After what feels like ten minutes but probably wasn't even one, he answers.

"You're levelheaded. I've always liked that about you. And I think what you're doing is admirable, for the record."

I hang on to the word "always." Did he even notice me in high school?

"Thanks," I say, tucking my hair behind my ears bashfully. "Just trying to do the right thing."

"Well, I'm a lawyer, not a businessman, so my version of the right thing might be different from yours But I'm a strong believer in trusting your gut."

He takes his eyes off the road for just a moment to lock eyes with me, his mouth curving into a soft smile. He is so handsome, that I can't hold his gaze for more than a moment. "Tell me about your life in Chicago," I say, hoping my attempt at small talk isn't as awkward as it sounds.

"What would you like to know?" His gaze remains on the road, which is good, because every time he looks at me with that compelling blue stare, my belly does this weird flipping thing.

I drum my fingers on my thighs. "Oh, I don't know. Hotshot lawyer, living it up as a bachelor in the city. Different woman every night of the week. It sounds awfully glamorous."

He lets out a short laugh. "I don't know about all that. Mostly it's just a lot of work."

"But you enjoy it?"

At this, he nods once, firm, like he doesn't even have to consider my question. "I enjoy the challenge, yes. But most nights I don't leave the office until nine thirty or ten. Sometimes later. If I'm lucky, I get home and nuke myself a frozen meal, half the time falling asleep on my couch before the damn thing's done cooking."

I smile at the thought of this. The ultra-handsome, hardworking, young attorney passed out with his tie loosened around his neck, his dinner uneaten in the kitchen. It paints an interesting picture, and one I wasn't expecting. Most men would have tried to impress me, telling tall tales about their conquests—inside the conference room, as well as the bedroom. But not Barrett. He's one-hundred percent genuine, and I like that more than I should.

We're back to the silence with a few more miles to go, so I opt for the radio in lieu of more tough questions. Barrett must have had the same idea because my fingers brush his on the dial.

"Sorry." I pull my hand away and turning back to the window to conceal my blushing cheeks. I'd like to chalk the jolt of electricity between our two hands up to static from the radio, but I can't lie to myself like that.

I place my fingertips, warm and buzzing, against my bottom lip, wondering if that "trust your gut" advice applies here, too. Because everything inside me is telling me to mount Barrett like a stallion and ride the ever-loving daylights out of him.

Chapter Five

Barrett

I've never been so glad to see a cheesy party store in my life.

Even with the frost creeping up the windows, the truck is getting a little too hot to handle with Ava sitting right next to me. I do my best to act casual, pulling into a parking spot, and ignoring the growing outline in my loose sweatpants while I kill the engine. When Ava reaches for her door, I take the chance to adjust myself so the bulge is less visible, trusting that my jacket will cover up the rest. The cold air is another welcome distraction, and I snag a cart from outside before pushing it in slowly through the door behind Ava. At this point, I need every opportunity for the cold weather to temper down my physical reaction to this woman.

Once inside, we fill the cart with clear glass vases, bouquets of flowers, and some paper lanterns. Ava is efficient and focused, and I'm grateful that this errand isn't going to turn into an all-day affair. Not that I'd mind spending extra time with her, but every second we're alone is one more second I'm berating my dick to behave while silently begging for this woman to get on my cock.

Fucked up, I know.

After we round up everything we need, I roll the cart up to the register and pull out my wallet. Ava is halfway through grabbing her card out of her purse when she catches me.

"You are *not* paying for this," she protests. "Just because you have a fancy lawyer job in the city doesn't mean you have to cover everything."

"That's not why." I place my card on the counter even as Ava narrows her eyes. "Your dad's always done a lot for me. I just want to give something back."

She's quiet for a second, thinking it over. I flash her a smile, hoping that a little extra encouragement will tip the scales in my favor. Her parents really have done a lot for me.

"Half." Ava places her card next to mine. "We'll split it."

It's not even that much money, but if it makes her feel better, I'm willing to let her win this one. "Alright, deal."

After we pay I roll the cart back out, and the chill has really set in. A fresh layer of snow blankets the parking lot, covering the windshield of the truck, and there's ice spreading out from the sidewalk out across the asphalt.

What a mess.

"Wait inside," I say.

"Why?" She hoists the bag in her arms a bit higher, fighting off the chill.

"Because I'm going to load everything up and bring the truck back over. It's wet and cold, which is a recipe for slipping on your ass which I've seen you do plenty over your lifetime."

"And you're immune to slipping on your ass?" Her eyes flicker, meeting mine with a challenge.

"It's easier for me to carry everything at once. I'll do it in one trip and drive the truck back. Three minutes tops."

"Are you serious right now? You want to carry all eight of these bags? You can drop the macho act."

She's acting like I'm treating her like a delicate flower, but I'm just trying to be a gentleman. "It's not an act."

"So, you act like a nineteen-fifties husband with everyone, then?" She puts down her bag, making a grab for her purse instead. "I'll call Nick and ask about that."

The last thing I want is Nick getting any idea that I'm being sweet on his sister. "Ava, come on. It's freezing out. I'm just trying to help."

"I'm going to be running a factory full of men," she counters swiftly, but abandons her search for the phone to look me in the eyes, "I know how to deal with an ego."

I raise a brow, daring her to continue about the size of my *ego*, and anger flares across her face before she storms off the sidewalk toward the truck with three bags of streamers and paper plates hanging on her arms over her marshmallow puff coat. Cursing under my breath, I follow close behind her with the rest of the bags. Ava doesn't make it three stomping steps before her shoe slips on a patch of ice, and she topples backwards.

She tries to turn and catch herself, but I'm close enough that she grabs at me for purchase. There's a harsh tug on my sweatpants, and the momentum takes them right down to my ankles, freezing air suddenly whips across my skin. Ava falls all the way to her knees, looking up as I look down. It's cold as hell, but that doesn't stop a blush from rising all the way to her hairline, as she tries to keep her eyes on mine instead of the front of my black boxer briefs.

"You know, if you wanted an encore of last night you just could have asked," I say, and it's impossible not to grin.

"It was an accident," she mumbles, clearing her throat as if it will hide the heat on her cheeks. The parking lot is practically abandoned, but the idea of someone seeing us is enough for Ava to break her iron grip on my sweatpants and try to find her bearings on the ice again. I bend to yank my pants back up, grateful that the cold is keeping me in check.

I hold my hand out to help her up. She glares at me, but it only lasts a few seconds before she grabs my hands with both of hers, and I lift her up to her feet. When her shoes scrape on the snow, I put my free hand against her back, sandwiching us with party supplies and pulling her close so she doesn't slip again and escort her to the truck.

The weather has turned fast, and I want her safely inside the truck. We toss the bags inside, and I help her climb up.

"There. Safe and sound." I grin. "If only you'd listened to me in the first place, the fine customers at Shop-N-Save wouldn't have seen me in my underwear."

She shrugs. "I don't like being told what to do unless I'm naked."

I don't like being told what to do unless I'm naked?

Eyes widening, I shake my head at her. Damn, she's definitely grown up. I don't remember her ever being this sassy, and fuck, I like it. I shut her door and climb into the driver's seat.

I start the truck, and clean the windshield, and after I do, I realize Ava is still watching me.

"Barrett?" she asks, voice soft.

I know what she's asking. What is this? What's happening between us? But I'm fresh out of answers. This chemical attraction that's building between us is big and electrifying. And fucking terrifying, because there's no way we can act on it.

My gaze lowers from her eyes to her full, kissable lips, and suddenly all I can think about is kissing her. Taking her plush mouth with mine…Imagining what she'd look like undressed for me. Ass raised up, her hips the perfect height to grip in my hands, pulling her back onto my stiff length, hearing her cry out as I penetrate her fully for the first time.

I take a deep breath and begin to mentally calculate my billable hours from last month, recite the Latin names for legal concepts I studied in law school, anything to stop myself from doing the one thing I want to do—kissing all that sexual frustration right off her beautiful lips.

Her gaze falls to my mouth, and the moment it does, it's all I can think about. Goodbye, habeas corpus. Hello, lust.

Ava wets her lower lip with her tongue and in an instant, I've closed the distance between us, bringing my lips to hers in a searing kiss.

The moment our mouths meet, she lets out a sound of surprise, but from the way she tilts her head up to meet mine, it's a welcome one. I linger as long as I dare, not wanting to give up her sweet lips, her little breathless sounds just yet. Denying myself that would feel like death.

"We really shouldn't be doing this," I murmur with my lips still lingering against hers, because it seems like the right thing to say.

She kisses me again. It's hot and insistent, her hands grasping at my coat before she answers with a smile. "I know that."

I can think of plenty of ways to heat her up a couple more degrees, but unfortunately, we're in her father's truck in the middle of a parking lot. Taking herculean strength, I pull back from her, certain that guilt is written all over my face. I can't even look her in the eye at this point, all I see are the remnants of my sins reflected on my best friend's sister's face. Her splotched cheeks, the lust-filled eyes, the swollen lips, or maybe that's what I'm seeing in my own reflection. Fuck. "Nice as this is, we should probably get back to the house."

She nods, and I pull out onto the road when the full-force of what we've done hits me. I *kissed* Ava. I kissed her without even thinking about it, after spending years trying to put her out of my mind. Worse, I called it *nice*. The opportunity was there, and everything in me wanted to take advantage. If she hadn't kissed me back, I would have stopped. But, man, she did kiss me back and it was everything I'd imagined. Hot, soft, sweet.

"Shit." Ava startles when I curse, and I resist the urge to reach over and touch her in some small way. "None of this was supposed to happen."

"Nothing *did* happen," she says back, so casually I can barely believe it. "Which is why we're going to unpack the truck when we get back home and go on with our day."

I force a breath into my lungs. At least that means Nick won't have to find out. I couldn't risk my oldest friend in the world hating me because of one stupid mistake.

I nod, staring straight out the windshield, like there could possibly be anything more interesting outside than the woman next to me.

With every passing minute, the silence strains into awkwardness, and I reach over to flip the radio on. Ava's hand doesn't brush mine this time, instead staying locked in her lap. A jazzy beat flows from the speakers; it's not my type of music, but this is more about drowning out the silence than hearing the latest top forty.

When the house comes into view, I hold back a breath of relief, and pull into the driveway without breaking the quiet between us. Nick is outside already, scraping off the front porch with a snow shovel, and the bastard waves as soon as we get out. His wave is like a sucker punch to the gut. If he finds out how close I was to violating his sister, I have a very good feeling that that wave would turn into a right hook.

"Took you two long enough." He kicks the last bit of snow off the concrete, then leaves the shovel by the door. "Did you make a detour or something?"

Neither one of us answers, and when I loop around to grab the bags, Ava stops in front of me.

For a second, I'm not sure whether to go around, or take a step back and let her by. We stare at each other until Nick raises an eyebrow.

"What's going on? Do you both want to freeze your asses off out here?"

"No, he told me to wait insi-" Ava starts.

"I didn't want her to slip again and-" I interrupt, and she gives me a pleading look.

Nick rolls his eyes. "Yeah, okay. How about we get inside? It's freezing balls out here."

"Fine by me," I say hastily, passing off the lightest bag to Ava.

She glances inside it, seeing the paper lanterns, and sighs. "I guess I'll go try to figure out how to assemble these before Mom and Dad get back."

She walks past Nick without another word and into the house. I haul everything else up to the porch, turning back to head to the truck and close the door. I pause as Nick taps me on the shoulder.

"Did Ava say something to piss you off?" Nick asks, sounding none too surprised. "Everything that's happened with Dad has left her kind of moody."

Hoisting the bags back into my arms, I give him a look. "No, man, she's fine. It's just weird to catch up after so long."

Thankfully, he doesn't even blink at the lie. "Well, at least she's not driving you crazy. I wish she would just give up on this whole factory thing and instead get on with her own life."

I thought she did have a life here, but a creak from behind catches my attention. Ava is standing in the doorway with her arms crossed, irritation tight between her brows.

I can tell by her expression that she heard every bit of that.

"Thanks for the support, Nick." Sarcasm cuts through her tone, quick and sharp.

"Listen, I'm on your side, okay?" He puts his hands up like it'll ward her off. "That scrapheap shouldn't be anyone's business anymore. Even Barrett knows it's not worth your time."

Ava stares at me, looking surprised and hurt all at once, and I rush to clarify, "That's not what I said. It's your decision, Ava."

"But I think a lawyer knows a good deal when he sees one," Nick insists.

I shrug. "If Ava says she can handle it, then she can handle it. Your dad put a lot of work into that place."

"Yeah, whatever." Stubborn or not, Nick tends to back down when he's outnumbered.

"Thank you, *Barrett*," Ava says, deliberately emphasizing my name.

After a quick nod, I move to take the rest of the bags inside. She steps back out of the way, body just inches from mine, and I tell myself to keep on walking.

But not before one last phrase jettisons into my head out of the depths of my subconscious sins.

'Mens rea.'

A guilty mind…how fucking appropriate.

Chapter Six

Ava

It's a wonder my mother lets me help in the kitchen anymore. Her off-script cooking style and my dedicated loyalty to the recipe mix about as well as oil and vinegar— our evening of cookie baking made that clear yet again. With Dad, her usual sous chef, napping off his long morning of doctors' appointments, she's stuck with me and my slow but methodical process of slicing peppers in perfectly even slices.

"It's all getting mixed up in a salad anyway," she reminds me. "It doesn't matter if they're even or not."

I accept the reminder with a smile but keep at my slow, precise work. After all, if I focus all my energy on this, maybe I won't completely lose my mind over the master chef to my immediate left.

Barrett, playing the part of the perfect house guest, dices and chops vegetables along with me. Helping even though he's not even staying for dinner tonight. I'm careful to stand a solid foot to his side as not to run the risk of my arm brushing his, afraid of how visibly obvious it would be to Mom that just the brush of this man's arm would send me into a state of euphoria. A kiss turned me on my head for over an hour. Still, watching his hands at work out of the corner of my eye is enough for me to wish he'd handle me with that kind of skill.

Something about a man who knows his way around the kitchen turns me on quicker than you can preheat an oven. Or maybe it's just the way he cradles that cucumber, wrapping his large hand around it one finger at a time. Am I imagining things, or is Barrett holding that cucumber a little lewdly on purpose?

When I lift my gaze, the smug grin on his face gives me my answer. He runs his hand down the cucumber twice in a slow, stroking motion and my cheeks flush. He's made a game out of teasing me, and there's nothing I can do but play along. I roll my eyes in his direction, thankful that it seems to break the awkward tension from earlier today. But the second Mom turns her back to load dishes into the dishwasher, Barrett presses what I hope is a cucumber against my outer thigh and leans in close enough that his breath teases the hair on my neck.

I stop breathing, fearing if I make a sound that Mom will turn around and catch this, us, whatever this is.

"Stop staring, Ava," he murmurs. His bottom lip barely grazes my ear lobe and a rush shoots through me. "We both know you couldn't handle this."

My God, please tell me that it's a cucumber up against my thigh and not his dick. I can't even bring myself to look down, only straight ahead. I'm pretty much positive it isn't a cucumber. If I make eye contact with Barrett, I'm going to push everything off this damn counter and beg him for it, cucumber or not.

A wave of heat continues to pulse through me at the realization of his words. I hate to admit that he just might be right. If what I saw when Barrett stepped out of the shower was any indication, he might split me in half with one thrust. He might be too much for me to take, but why does every inch of him make me want to try?

"Need any help?"

The sound of Mom's voice jolts Barrett back into behaving. Tossing the cucumber back on the cutting board, he resumes dinner prep as if we hadn't just been teetering on the edge of foreplay in my mother's kitchen.

"Don't worry, Mrs. Saunders. I've got everything under control."

If by *everything* he means me, then yes, he absolutely does. To say I'm putty in his hands is an understatement. He's got a grip on me tighter than the one he just had on that cucumber. At this point, I know there's no way I can sit through a family dinner without groping Barrett's dick under the table as he passes me the salad dressing. Because I am shameless and cannot stop thinking about his cucumber. Which he really needs to keep to himself.

Turning away from my recipe duties, I snag my phone out of my back pocket while Mom and Barrett are discussing the rest of the menu and shoot off an emergency text to my best friend Megan, praying she's not busy. Luckily, she responds in an instant, asking if she needs to call and fake a death in the family. A snicker escapes the side of my mouth. She's always had my back no matter what.

"What's so funny, Ava?" Mom asks as both she and Barrett turn to look at me, a smirk all over his gorgeous face.

"Oh, nothing. It's just Megan. She actually needs me to meet her at the mall. It seems kind of urgent, plus I should pick up a present for Dad anyway. Two birds, one stone. Save me a plate?"

I have one arm in my coat before she even has the time to respond. Barrett shoots me a "I know exactly what you're doing" look, but I brush it off and breeze out the door without another word. It feels good to be back in the driver's seat of my car, back in a position of control for the first time in the past twenty-four hours.

When I turn the key in the ignition, the engine sputters and then goes silent. This has got to be a joke. I give it a few more desperate tries, but it does nothing but leave my fingers stiff and cold in my gloves. *Shit.* I'm going to have to go back in there. Stepping back into the concentrated sexual tension I left unresolved in the kitchen isn't exactly a safe move for me, but if I grab the keys to Dad's truck quick enough, I might be able to slip out without notice.

As quietly as I can muster, I crack open the door and tiptoe toward where all the keys are stored near the back of the kitchen.

"Back so soon, sweetie?" Mom asks.

Well, it was worth a shot.

"Yeah, my car wouldn't start. I'll just take Dad's truck, no worries."

Mom crinkles her face in disapproval. "I don't know if I trust the truck with the roads being this bad, Ava."

"I can give you a lift," Barrett suggests, chopping up the last of the cucumbers. "I was going to head out soon anyway. I told my mom I'd come over for dinner tonight."

Mom's face softens into a pleased smile at Barrett's offer. "I'd feel much better about that, Ava."

"Sure, that's fine," I say, not opposed to another opportunity to let my eyes wander Barrett's sculpted frame without my mother as our audience.

"I'll leave the front door unlocked for you tonight, Barrett," Mom says, giving his forearm a grateful squeeze. "And thank your mom again for sharing you with us. It's been so nice to have the extra set of hands helping out around the house."

God, if only those hands could help me out, too.

* * *

Once we're inside the car, Barrett turns up the heat and adjusts the vents to direct some of the warm air toward me.

"I'm sorry about what you overheard with Nick before. I meant what I said about supporting you in whatever you want to do. If saving the plant is your goal, then that's pretty fucking commendable."

"It's honestly fine. Thank you, though." I shrug him off. It's been no surprise that Nick's against my plan. Ever since his quickie wedding and even faster divorce, he's been in a sour mood. Just because his dreams fell through doesn't mean he can't be happy for the rest of us.

The mall parking lot is packed to the brim, but I could spot Megan's bright red hair from a mile away. She's leaning against a pillar by the front entrance, scanning the parking lot for any car that looks familiar. I sent off a warning text on the way to let her know I'd be dropped off in front, but I didn't mention who would be doing the driving. Too much to try to explain via text without Barrett asking what I was typing so furiously about. I direct him toward Megan and he pulls up the car, shifting it into park.

"I can pick you up tonight," he offers.

"I'm sure Megan can drive me home." One-on-one car rides with Barrett, plus the cover of darkness? That's a dangerous combination that I might not be able to resist.

Outside my window, Megan tilts her head in an effort to identify my mysterious driver. Could she be any less subtle? When I open the door, her eyes light up with recognition as she gets a clear look at my chauffeur.

"Oh, my—"

I cut her off with a tight squeeze of her wrist. "Thanks again for the ride," I call over my shoulder as I tug Megan away from the car and into the warm safety of the mall.

"I'm sorry, was that or was that not Barrett Wilson?" Her eyes are wide like she just spotted an A-list celebrity, not my high-school heartthrob.

"The one and only," I say, a smirk tugging at the sides of my lips.

"Since when are you guys a thing? God, I didn't think it was possible, but he's gotten more gorgeous. Didn't you have a major crush on him in high school?"

"We're not a *thing*." I pause, then hand over the gossip I know she so desperately wants. "Although we may have kissed."

Saying it out loud leaves my lips warm and buzzing, almost as good as the kiss itself. I haven't felt like this about a man in such a long time, but of all people, does it really have to be my brother's best friend?

"You are so lucky the mall is open late," she says, "because you have a ton of explaining to do."

As we weave in and out of stores in search of a fitting retirement gift for my dad, I fill her in on every detail. The shower ordeal, the standoff followed by the pantsing accident, all of it. She cackles at my horrible luck, and I can't really blame her. The past few days have been nothing short of a parade of embarrassing moments, but I'd take a hundred more slip-ups if it meant Barrett would kiss me like that one more time. I'm clearly insane.

"So, what's next? Is 'present shopping for my dad' code for 'picking out new lingerie'?" She gestures toward a lingerie store, raising her eyebrows suggestively. I'm ashamed to say it takes me a second to rule out the idea. The thought of Barrett pulling something black and lacy off me with his teeth is almost enough for me to abandon any ounce of the self-control I've been clinging to. Key word: almost.

"He's Nick's best friend, Megan. Nothing can happen. That would be like if you and Nick hooked up."

She purses her lips and shrugs, her eyes pointed at the ceiling. "You're right, I'd never go there," she teases, which earns her a swat on the arm. I duck into a store filled with greeting cards and Megan follows me.

"But come on, Ava. You're not passing this up. This is Barrett we're talking about here. Every high school fantasy we ever had come to life. And it's not like you're on the market for anything serious, right?"

I shake my head. "Taking over the plant is taking over my life. I don't have the time to maintain a relationship right now. Plus, he's in Chicago. Dating a guy who lives three hours away is only something I would have done in college. Our lives don't line up. More than that, my brother would disown one of us if he ever found out." I'm not sure who I'm trying to convince, her or myself.

"So, then, what does it matter?" she asks, rolling her eyes and flipping halfheartedly through a stack of retirement cards. "You're adults. And you have chemistry. You don't have to live by some high school 'bro code.' And it's not like you share the details of your sex life with your brother. What he doesn't know isn't going to hurt him."

I don't know what to say, so I just shake my head. Chemistry or no chemistry, I could never just throw caution to the wind like that. It's not me. Even if I might want it to be.

"You get what you want and then you go your separate ways. No harm, no foul." Her mouth curls into a devilish grin. "And if he's ever back in town, well, there's no shame in going back for seconds."

Chapter Seven

Barrett

The drive over to my mother's house is a lot longer than I remember.

I could speed things up, lay on the gas and be there a few minutes sooner, but more than anything I want to turn right around and head to Ava's place. *Her* mother would welcome me back in with open arms, and I wouldn't have to worry about taking up too much space. Frustration burns slowly in my chest like a slow wildfire when I spy the sign for my old neighborhood, making a tight turn down the snow-slick road.

I blow out a slow breath. A few hours of smiling and talking to everybody, catching up because no one ever calls, or sends birthday cards, then I can drive on back before it's too late. Of course, I love my family, but I've always been the odd one out, the firstborn son before my mom was married, and hardly out of high school. When I was seven years old, she married Bob and had another family. One I've never quite felt part of. Now, every time we're around each other, I can't fight the feeling that I'm overstaying my welcome.

Cars crowd the driveway as I pull up, and I have to snag a space farther down the street, right on the edge of the neighbor's property. Ice crunches under my feet on my way to the front but it's nothing like the noise I can hear filtering through the door, half a dozen voices all talking over each other.

I knock as a warning before stepping inside, since the door is never locked. "How's it going, everyone?"

Both of my half-siblings have taken custody of the living room couch, chatting among themselves, but my two nieces wave when they see me. "Hi, Uncle Barrett!"

"Barrett?" My mother's voice carries from the kitchen. "Come say hi, sweetie."

It's a short walk through the living room to find her, and I have to duck under one of the pans hanging from the rack on the ceiling. Everything is jammed tight between the counter and the stove; half the cabinets open for ingredients, so she has everything in reach. She's balancing her attention between three different pots at once, and I'm standing there for a few seconds before my presence catches her attention.

"Hi, honey." Our eyes meet for just a moment before Mom turns back to the stove and stirs something. It looks like the same soup she used to make when we were all squeezed in under one roof; the more ingredients, the better. "Just give me one second."

Waiting there with my hands in my pockets, it's impossible not to feel awkward. I miss the Saunders' place already, teasing Ava while doing my part to help cook. It felt warm, like a home, and I instantly miss that feeling of watching her eyes light up while I talk to her. Here, I can barely breathe past the steam and too many smells colliding in the small space.

Mom breaks away from the food just long enough to pull me into a polite hug, arms loose against the stiffness of my back. "I'm sorry we didn't have any space for you to stay this time with your old bedroom being turned into an office and all. I barely had enough chairs for dinner."

That explains the metal fold-out one by the living room table. "Don't worry about it, Mom. At least we get to eat together, right?"

"Right." Her smile doesn't quite reach her eyes when she pulls away from me.

I return to the living room and sit down with the intention of trying to make small talk, but the conversation is dominated by my two toddler nieces, so I settle for smiling and watching them play on the floor. My half-brother Jonathan and his wife are bickering, and my half-sister Kimberly seems more interested in playing on her phone than catching up.

Mom calls my name from the kitchen, and I'm happy to escape the awkwardness and lend a hand.

When I enter behind her, she's wiping her hands on a towel and surveying her work.

"Dinner is just about ready. Can you help me carry some of these dishes into the dining room? And then call everybody over to the table so we can get started?"

Things have felt different ever since my stepdad passed away a few years ago, and I wish I could wrap my mom in a big hug and ask her if she's really okay. But I know she'd just give me a look and say of course. So, I don't. Instead, I head into the living room and announce that dinner's ready.

It takes a few minutes of wrangling to get everyone in their chairs, especially since mine is backed against the corner. My nieces sit on either side, leaning forward so they can talk to each other, but Jonathan seems more occupied with the beer he just snagged from the fridge than any kind of dinner conversation. When Kimberly sits down, I notice a new ring on her finger.

"Kimberly, did you get engaged?" I ask.

She seems surprised that I noticed, but instantly lights up with excitement. "It was right over the holiday. Roger finally asked me, which is a relief, because I thought he never would."

Jonathan chuckles to himself. "That's another one tied down in the family. You better start catching up, Barrett."

"We're not all running on the same path with the same end goal in mind," I say, biting my tongue against another comment when Mom comes over with piping hot bowls of soup. Jonathan got married at twenty-one, and it seems Kimberly won't be far behind him.

"Does the firm still have you working those long hours?" Mom frowns, taking her seat between my siblings. "They should really think about people trying to get settled in with their lives and with family."

"I'm settled, Mom. If you came down to Chicago sometime and saw my place, you'd know that for sure."

"She's worried because you're the oldest," Jonathan mutters, into the opening of his beer bottle.

"There's nothing to worry about," I counter firmly.

Kimberly runs a thumb fondly over her engagement ring before looking at me. "But isn't it lonely? Being all by yourself in that big city."

I almost blurt out that I feel more alone boxed into this corner than I ever have in the city. How many people there are surrounding you doesn't really matter when it comes to feeling welcome. And as for Kimberly? Maybe I'm just bitter, but the fact that her fiancé isn't even here tonight speaks volumes.

"No. It's exactly what I need." Searching for a distraction from the subject, I dig into my dinner, but even after the silverware starts clattering, everyone's eyes stay on me. "Honestly, I don't even have time. Besides, why would I stop at the middle of the ladder and get married when I can climb all the way to the top?"

As soon as the words have left my mouth, I know the sentiment will be lost on them.

"Because you're in your thirties now, Barrett." Mom sighs. "I can't remember the last time you told me about a special woman in your life."

I stare at her in disbelief. This house was so crowded that she doesn't even have a place for me to sleep, or a real spot at the table, and yet I'm supposed to bring a wife and kids back home? They wouldn't feel like they belonged any more than I do.

"The girls are getting into gymnastics," Jonathan chimes in, and my mom's entire face lights up as she leans in to ask them questions about it.

My nieces happily babble on either side of me, as if I wasn't there at all. When my mom promises to come to their first practice, an ache settles deep in my chest. I had years of games, and she hardly managed to come to any of them. I'm not sure if she's telling the truth, or making another promise she can't keep.

I tell myself it doesn't matter.

Kimberly catches me frowning, and flashes a kind smile my way. She's the youngest out of all of us and was never anything but sweet, except we grew up so many years apart that there never seemed to be anything to talk about. With a wedding waiting in the wings, I imagine that's the only subject on her mind right now. So, I opt for ending the awkwardness and bring that subject up with her.

"So, how's wedding planning going?"

"Roger said we'll send out invitations as soon as we decide on a date." Her smile widens, turning hopeful. "Do you think you could come? It'd be great to have the whole family there."

I nod without even thinking. "If I can get the time off, of course I'll come."

"And if you have a plus one by then, just let me know. I'll throw in an extra," Kimberly says, and I have to hold in a groan.

Everyone's so eager to turn their futures over to a picket fence and two-point-five kids. I love my nieces, but

I know Jonathan is locked into some middle management job that he hates, and will be for at least another decade to get the two of them through school.

Nick couldn't keep things together either, and he jumped at the chance to get married. Now I'm not sure if he was in love with his ex or if he just got caught up in the moment and thought it was the right thing to so. Shouldn't a lifelong promise matter more? Shouldn't it be built on a foundation that's never going to break?

That's what I'm building at the firm, and I'm getting so close to reaching that goal. My coach would never let me give up back in college, and I'm sure as hell not giving up now. Even if it means everyone eyeing me for flying solo at the dinner table for the next few years.

"Who wants to help with dishes?" My mom asks, and my sister-in-law immediately moves back to the couch in the living room, clearly still frustrated with Jonathan.

"I got it, Mom," Jonathan says, getting up from his seat. "Want to dry for me, Kim? It'll be like old times again."

"Yeah, sure." Kimberly stands up, too, then glances back at me. "Could you toss the trash out, Barrett? I'm pretty sure the bag's about to burst."

It's a chance to step out and get a breather, so I nod and work my way out from behind the table. I haul the bag outside to the can, and for a second, I stand out in the cool air, looking at the light coming from the house.

I could leave right now. I'm not sure if anyone would even say anything if I did, or if it would be the new family drama passed around the next set of brief holiday phone calls. The only thing really stopping me is that my mom might get upset. At the end of the day, she's still my mother, and I don't want to hurt her.

I take a deep breath and shove the trash bag into the bin. After kicking the ice off my shoes, I step back into the house, holding the door so the wind doesn't slam it shut. Mom is in the living room with the girls, but I can hear Jonathan and Kimberly talking together in the kitchen.

"Is Barrett even really into women?" Jonathan mutters, his next few words covered up by a dish splashing into the sink. "I'm starting to wonder."

"Jonathan, that's rude," Kimberly protests. "It's his life, you know?"

"I'm just saying, if I looked like he did, I'd have a woman on each arm. He's a lawyer in a big city, and still doesn't have anyone to show for it."

Both of my hands clench into tight fists, frustration almost drowning out Kimberly's next words. "Maybe there was a bad break-up he didn't tell us about or something."

Everything in me wants to walk into the kitchen and ask why anything I do is their business, but I hold back. This isn't the place to start a family fight, especially when I do my best to keep my nose out of their lives. You'd think they'd extend me the same courtesy.

"Barrett, are you staying for dessert?" Mom asks, forcing my attention away from the conversation in the other room.

"I should probably get going so I don't wake up the Saunders coming back in." Somehow, I manage a smile, not wanting to worry her at the last minute. "Leaves more for the girls to eat anyway."

When my nieces cheer, I take that as a victory. Mom returns my smile, but doesn't get up from the couch next to my still pouting sister-in-law to give me another hug. Taking a step closer to the kitchen, I call out to Jonathan and Kimberly.

"Night, everyone!"

Porcelain clanks against steel as one of them almost drops a dish. From the low curse afterwards, it's my brother. "Catch you later, Barrett."

"Have a good night," Kimberly adds, sounding as embarrassed as he does.

Without hesitation, I step back out into the snow. It's a long walk back to my car at the end of the street, but as soon as I'm behind the wheel, I hit the gas. This house is the last place I want to be, especially when the people who actually want me in this town are only a few miles away.

Chapter Eight

Ava

I can't say for certain what it was that woke me. Maybe it was the uneasy feeling deep in my stomach that something was off. It's more likely, however, that it was Barrett's headlights shining directly through my bedroom window. Either way, I haven't been asleep long and now that I'm up, I'm wide awake.

I reach over to my nightstand to check the time on my phone—it's pushing midnight, which seems awfully late considering Barrett was visiting his mom just a few neighborhoods over. The low purr of his engine halts and I sit up in bed, trying to quiet my breath to listen for the sound of the doorknob turning or the garage door going up.

A minute passes, then another, but there's no sound other than my heart pounding against my chest, which seems so deafening that I'm sure it will wake the entire house. Another minute and still not a sound. My head starts running through scenarios. Maybe Mom forgot to leave the front door unlocked. Another minute comes and goes in silence before I toss back the covers and push my feet into my slippers. If I can't sleep, I might as well investigate.

I'm not exactly dressed to impress in my oversized sweatshirt, and pink pajama pants, but the thought of Barrett freezing to death outside my parents' house takes precedence over my outfit. I pad down the steps and tug the front door open—Mom had left it unlocked for him after all, which eases my concern for his safety, but piques my interest as to what the hell he's doing out in the cold. It's almost too dark to see past the front steps, but if I squint, I can just barely make out his motionless silhouette in the driver's seat of his parked Audi.

The wind whips mercilessly against my cheeks, making every step down the icy driveway feel like a leap of faith, but I eventually make it to the passenger side of his car. After a single tap on the window, he turns his head, startled for just a second. I wiggle my fingers in a gentle wave and he unlocks the door. I take that as an invitation.

It's not much warmer inside since the car isn't running, but at least I'm out of the wind. I can't stop shivering, and for a while the only sound in the car is our quiet breathing. Sitting in silence in cars with Barrett. This is starting to become a trend.

There's a few seconds of silence, and then Barrett glances over at me. "I feel like there's so much we haven't caught up on."

"What would you like to know?"

He shrugs. "I don't know." He looks straight out the windshield, with a contemplative expression. "What' the most rebellious thing you've ever done?"

I wonder if he assumes that stealing a peek at his package, or kissing him would be high up on the list. And maybe they would, if I could bring myself to regret them.

"Probably skipping my economics class, the entire fall semester of my senior year. The professor only counted the mid-term and the final exam toward our grades, so I literally only went to class twice. I swear people were like who are you? Are you in the wrong classroom?" I smile remembering back, and then realize it's a little ridiculous that *this* is the most outrageous thing I've done. Maybe I should have lived more, maybe then I'd have tales about drunken spring break escapades or sky diving behind my parents' back. Instead I've always done what was expected of me, tried to be a good daughter, a good sister, a good friend.

"But you passed?" he asks.

I blink, realizing he's asking about the econ class. "I read the textbook. I knew the material, I just didn't see a point in sitting through the lectures for ninety minutes every week if I didn't have to."

He nods. "I would have been the same way in law school if I could have gotten away with it."

I like the image of a studious younger Barrett taking notes and volunteering commentary on his professor's lecture.

"What are you doing up?" he finally asks, as if me being awake this late is somehow more suspicious than him sitting out here in the cold.

"Your headlights...my bedroom window faces the driveway."

He rakes his fingers through his chestnut hair. "Shit, I'm sorry."

"Don't worry about it. I was having trouble sleeping anyway."

It's not entirely true, but it's enough for the embarrassed look on his face to subside. "I guess everyone's got a lot on their mind tonight then," he says.

"Is something wrong?"

"Nothing's wrong. Just needed some space to think through a few things."

"What kind of things?" I can feel my face soften and my heart sink just a little bit.

"Nothing specific."

He's as frustrating as he is gorgeous but I don't want to pry, so I tease him instead. "Does your knack for evading questions serve you well as a lawyer?"

The corners of his mouth hint at the slightest smile and he relaxes into his seat, releasing the white-knuckle grip he still had on the wheel.

"I've just been thinking about future plans and all that," he admits.

"So, you're a planner too."

"Maybe not as much as you are. What do you have laid out?"

I shrug, my shivers subsiding a little bit as our body heat warms the car. "After I whip the plant into shape — the plan is to settle down with the right guy in the next couple of years, enjoy each other for a while, then hopefully start a family by the time I'm thirty." I've repeated this plan so many times that it feels as natural as reciting the alphabet. I wasn't the kind of girl in high school who was pretty or popular, and in college I was busy double-majoring in business and accounting, it felt like there was never time for a relationship. After I graduated, I was focused on working. I decided last year that if I wanted to make it happen for myself, I needed to make finding a man a priority. And I will—as soon as I get the factory in order. I know what I want, and I'm mature enough now to be upfront about it.

Barrett studies me in the dark. I half expected him to roll his eyes, or tell me how cliché that was, but instead, he looks impressed. "You've got it all figured out, don't you?"

"Yeah, I guess I do. A lot of people think I'm crazy for having a checklist like this, but I want what I want," I say with another shrug. "What about you? What do you want?"

"To make partner at my law firm this year," he says firmly, not needing even a second to consider his answer. "I've been busting my ass and I'm on track. I work for what I want. I just can't do it with any distractions."

I feel the blood rush to my cheeks and am suddenly thankful that it's too dark for him to see me turn pink. Am I the kind of distraction he's talking about? Or am I the most rebellious thing he's done? I steer the conversation elsewhere to be safe. "How was your mom?"

"Fine," he says, although the strained tone of his voice says the opposite. "They're so different from me that I sometimes can't believe we're related. Talking to them about work is painful. If it's not about me getting married or having kids, they can't even pretend like they're impressed with the goals I'm working toward."

Maybe it's my lack of sleep, or maybe it's that we're covered in the kind of darkness that only Indiana winter nights can offer, but in a rare moment of bravery, I slide my hand over to squeeze Barrett's thigh.

"Different people value different things, Barrett. It's incredibly impressive what you've accomplished."

And now I wonder if maybe daring to be different from his family's expectations is actually the most rebellious thing he's done.

He twitches at my touch, the muscles in his thigh bunching beneath my gentle grip. I can hear his breath hitch just the slightest bit, but he keeps staring ahead. I should pull my hand away, my fingertips are close to dangerous territory, but I don't move an inch. And a delighted quiver runs through me.

I raise my eyes from where my hand rests against his leg, to the button of his jeans, to the smooth slope of his gorgeous jawline and full mouth.

He turns his head and the second our eyes lock, the heat that's been building between us all day floods over my cheeks and down my spine. Laying one tentative hand on the back of my neck, his fingers slid into the back of my hair, and my eyes sink closed. The moment pulses with electricity, and it's stronger than anything I've felt before.

Ever so slowly, Barrett leans closer as he pulls me in and presses his mouth to mine.

His lips are soft, yet firm, and he kisses just like he does everything else—confidently and with the skill of a man who knows exactly what he wants.

He cradles my jaw and tastes my bottom lip with his tongue. My lips part in gentle invitation and then his tongue meets mine in a dizzying rush.

One perfect, slow kiss becomes three or four quicker, deeper ones, and suddenly, I'm groaning my approval and giving myself over to what I've wanted for so long.

This moment is everything I've dreamed about for years, but never thought would actually happen. His tongue makes long, lazy strokes against mine, and my body tightens in anticipation, heart thundering in my chest.

Maybe he wasn't my first kiss, like I dreamed about all the years ago, but I wouldn't mind if he was my last.

He takes hold of my hips to pull me onto his lap. I settle against him, a little amazed that we fit like this. His car is a lot roomier than it seems.

His lips wander down my neck as I spread my thighs wider to surround either side of him. He's hard, his bulge pressing against me as I press my hands against his chest. He's so solid everywhere, and the desire to feel more of him is a sharp pulse of need.

Feeling brave, I trail my fingers down his chest, stopping only when I get to the waistband of his jeans. His abs tighten under my touch. I'm not sure if it's rebellion, or just temporary insanity, but I slide one hand down to unbutton him, to get another look at what I've been craving all weekend, and silently cheer to myself. Operation Anaconda is in full effect. But Barrett grabs my hand and plants soft kisses against my knuckles.

"What's your plan there?" he asks, mouth tilted with the hint of a smile.

I swallow, my throat working with the effort. "I just thought…I'm attracted to you, and I thought maybe you were…"

"I am."

We kiss again, slower this time until Barrett finally pulls away.

"But we can't," he whispers, although his tongue flirting with my ear seems to suggest otherwise.

"Why not?"

"I may have good self-control," he says, cupping my chin and turning my head to meet his hypnotic blue eyes. "But if my cock comes out, I will fuck you. And I can't do that."

He's so close, I can feel him right there, and still I want more. I shift my hips closer, rocking against him, earning me a choked sound of pleasure. *God, that sound . . .*

"We're both adults now. We can do whatever we want."

He shakes his head. "The bro-code rules are written in stone. And the rules are simple. It's understood that a bro never makes eye contact with another bro while eating a banana. A bro always takes a piss standing up. And speaking of pissing . . . a bro never uses a urinal that's right next to another bro."

I shift in his lap, still horny, and now also confused. "What are you talking about?"

His eyes latch onto mine and he licks his lower lip. "No sex with your bro's ex. And definitely no sex with your bro's sister."

I let out a frustrated groan. "That's the most ridiculous thing I've ever heard."

He lifts a shoulder. "I don't make the rules. I just try and abide by them."

His brain may be telling him that we can't explore this sexual chemistry, but his body? It wants me. Bad. He's rock hard between my legs, and I can't help but notice the way his gaze wanders between my mouth and my breasts, as if he can't decide which part of me he wants to kiss next.

I straighten my shoulders, thrusting my breasts out even more. *Fuck the patriarchal bro code.* "Well, there's no way I can get back to sleep now. I'm all worked up." Biting my lip, I summon all my feminine wiles. *God, do I even have feminine wiles?* I must, because he looks like he's about to explode. "I need to come, Barrett."

Still watching me, he lets out a ragged groan.

"You can either sit here, or you can help me," I purr in my most seductive voice. Part of the maturity I spoke about earlier is not being afraid to go after what I want. And right now, I want this sexy man.

"Fuck." He lets out a sharp exhale, and I feel like I've already won.

I press a kiss to his neck and rock against him, shifting my hips until I collide against the hard ridge of him with just the right amount of friction. A grunt of frustrated need rumbles in his chest, and it's the best sound in the entire world.

Before I have a chance to press against him again, he lifts me up just enough to slide my pajama pants down. One hand presses into the small of my back, and the other yanks my panties to the side and greets my clit with two confident fingers. I can't stop myself from letting out a moan, which he responds to with an approving grin.

"How fast can you come, Ava?" he asks, his voice impossibly tight.

"I—I'm not sure," I murmur.

My hips move over him as he draws lazy circles around my swollen flesh with expert fingers. His lips trail my neck with slow, wet kisses that become quicker and rougher as his fingers gradually gain speed.

God, I've wanted this since he arrived, hell, since the first time I laid eyes on him. Did I dream of us in a car in my parents' driveway? Maybe when we were still in school, but definitely not as adults. But with Barrett's fingers sweeping through my wetness in time with his lips on my collarbone, we could be anywhere in the world and it would still be perfect.

His fingers explore me while his thumb keeps up the work right where I need it, and all I can do is let my head fall forward and nestle in against his warm neck with a low hum of pleasure.

"Feel good?"

"God, yes."

As his thumb strokes me faster and faster, I can feel myself tense, my insides tightening, and I groan his name. "Barrett . . ."

"That's it," he whispers. "You going to come for me?"

Everything contracts and releases, and the heat that's been building inside fills me with perfect, utter bliss. He pushes his thick fingers deep inside me to feel me contract and squeeze him. Then my insides tighten impossibly harder, sending a bolt of hot electricity coursing through me. I hang on to him, fixed on his deep blue eyes as he watches me in wonder.

He groans, his eyes on mine as I come and come for what seems like forever. "Fuck . . . that pussy is so nice and tight."

When my climax finally subsides, Barrett removes his fingers from my panties, and I see him bite his lip, fighting with himself.

I guess he wasn't kidding when he said he worked for what he wanted. He earned every bit of that, and from the cocky grin on his face, he knows it, but I'll be damned if I don't give him something in return.

I push my hips back down against his and begin rocking back and forth, which pulls a deep rumble from the back of Barrett's throat. I can feel him getting harder each time I thrust. Even through his jeans, I can feel how huge he is, far bigger than I expected, even given my sneak preview. His firm erection pressed between my legs is practically heaven, but I want more. No, I *need* more.

Maybe I could persuade his pants open after all, and then…

And then I would be fucking my brother's best friend. In the driveway.

The thought hits me like a snowball to the lady bits.

"Fuck," he groans again. "You have no idea how bad I've wanted this, but we can't and you know that as well as I do."

I pull back in a jolt of reality, and nod somberly.

Now that the endorphins have cleared, I can't believe what we just did—in my parents' freaking driveway of all places. I pull up my pants, and rush to open the car door.

"Ava, relax" he orders, laying one comforting hand on my shoulder. "No one has to know. It'll be okay."

I sweep his hand away. "Goodnight, Barrett." I don't add, thanks for the orgasm which was amazing until about thirty seconds ago. Instead, I fling open the door and the cold air fills the car that we warmed up all on our own. I didn't realize that we had fogged up the windows. God, how cliché. The driveway is too icy to run, but the second I'm in the house, I pound up the stairs as fast as my legs can carry me, running away from what was probably an enormous mistake.

I slip back into bed, but it isn't until I hear the sound of him shutting the front door that I finally take a breath. There. It's done. Closed. The door I never should have opened in the first place. But as much as I try to pretend no damage has been done, Barrett's voice, deep and sweet, echoes in my head all night. "No one has to know."

Of course, no one has to know. No one can *ever* know.

Chapter Nine

Barrett

When I wake up in the morning, the sun is shining brightly through the blinds, and I know instantly that I've overslept.

My alarm must have given up, because it's still blinking on my phone as I rub the sleep out of my eyes. For a second, I just sit up and listen, expecting the rest of the house to be up and awake without me, but there's nothing but silence. Which might be a good thing, I could use a moment to clear my head after what happened last night with Ava.

Wanting her is the equivalent of running with scissors. In a word, she's dangerous. Wanting her this desperately could put an end to the closest friendship I've got, and worse than that, I sense she could leave me brokenhearted. I don't have time for a relationship, even if I wanted one.

But that didn't stop Ava from filtering through every dream I had last night, the way she gasped and grabbed at my shoulders, burying her face in my neck, how slick and hot she was against my fingers. We could have gone so much farther, but she pulled away and managed to stop, and somehow, I did, too, even though everything in me wanted to follow her back to her bedroom and make sure she was alright.

A couple of deep breaths get me back under control before I get out of bed. I head to the bathroom and splash some cold water on my face, and after washing up, I tug on a pair of pants and a shirt before heading down the stairs.

A distant sneeze catches me by surprise, and when I duck my head into the kitchen, Ava is there, wrapped up in a fleece robe. She's pressed close to the stove, watching over a steel kettle that's yet to boil, and a box of tea bags sits next to her on the counter.

God, why does she have to look so good in a pair of pajama pants—the same pajama pants I'd pulled down the night before—a fuzzy robe, and a messy bun? That's not normal, right?

"Morning," I say entering the kitchen.

She jumps a little, and immediately covers her mouth to try and muffle a second sneeze.

"You okay?" I close the distance between us, and stop just out of arm's reach.

"Yeah, I'm fine. It's nothing."

"Doesn't sound like nothing."

She pulls her robe tighter. "It's a little cold. No big deal."

It might not be a dig deal to her, but I don't like seeing her under the weather. "Did spending time in a cold car after being in the nice warm house make you sick?"

"Spending time in the car?" She raises an eyebrow, and I can't quite tell if she's annoyed or amused. "Is that what you call it?"

"Well, you came out to see me and..." I start.

She pokes my arm to interrupt, scoffing under her breath, "I came out there to make sure you were okay. Don't blame me for catching a cold, you jerk. Typical."

"That's not what I meant." I don't want to insist too loud, not when someone else could be in the house, but Ava catches onto my hesitation in an instant.

"Nick isn't here." Just that single statement is enough to make my shoulders relax, but I'm even more relieved when she adds, "he went with my parents to the pharmacy."

Right. Nick mentioned that yesterday. It completely slipped my mind.

"So, we're alone," I say.

"Yes, we're alone, but don't get any ideas." Ava turns back around to the stove as steam billows out of the kettle's spout, making a high-pitched squeal. "Last night things went too far."

"I know." Hell, I'd known that the entire time, but with her body against mine, I hadn't been able to hold back. "Ava, I'm not blaming you for anything. We just lost our heads."

"We..." she starts, then goes quiet for a minute. I think she might have been expecting me to argue with her.

She pours the water into a porcelain mug, but sneezes while trying to drop the tea bag inside. I catch the cup right before it gets knocked off the counter, ignoring the hot water that spills down over my knuckles.

"Shit." She closes her eyes, clearly embarrassed. "I'm sorry, Barrett."

"Don't be sorry." After wiping up the spilled water, I smile.

She's nervous around me, and after last night, hell, maybe she has the right to be. Clearly, we don't know how to control ourselves. But from here on out, it's my job to make sure we do.

"Remember when you were little, and your pet ra

bbit went to go live in the country?"

"Yeah." The memory of Bunny brings a smile to her lips.

"Well, this thing between us is a little like that. It's better for everyone if we just let this go."

Her brows pinch together. "Barrett, I'm not that naïve. I know Bunny died and my parents made up that story to protect me."

"Then let me protect you from this, too. We have to bury these urges. Nick would hate me, and with me living in Chicago, there's no way it can develop into more anyway. It would only end up ruining everything."

She nods, looking somberly at her teacup.

"Go back up to bed and rest? I'll handle the tea," I suggest.

"You don't have to do that," she says softly.

"I know, but I want to." I hold Ava's gaze for a long moment, watching the tense line of her jaw, itching to brush my fingers down the side of her face. "It's not a macho thing. You came outside to make me feel better, so can't I do the same thing now?"

She lets out a soft sigh, and nods. "That'd be great."

I take a step back so she can step away from the stove, which I turn off the moment she leaves. With the tea brewing, I start checking through the cabinets and fridge, looking for something else that might help, and strike the jackpot with some chicken soup. Thankfully it doesn't take very long to heat up, and I carry the bowl upstairs in one hand and the mug in the other.

It's a little strange to barge right into her room, but she's already propped up in bed when I nudge the door open. She takes the tea between both her hands when I offer it, but surprise lights up her face when I set the soup on the bedside table.

"Well, aren't you handy?" She clears a rasp from her throat, then takes a slow sip of the tea. "Thank you."

"My law degree had to be good for something, right?" I grin, not sure if she wants me to stay or get out of her space. "I push microwave buttons like a pro now."

She rolls her eyes. "I don't know about that, but you're sweet."

She takes a sip of her tea, and I want to kick my own ass for focusing on her lips as she drinks.

"Hey, Barrett." Her voice is so soft, I wonder if what I was thinking showed on my face. "Can you check in that drawer for some tissues? I think my mom stashed some in there last time I was sick."

"Yeah, of course," I say, grateful for the distraction.

The dresser is a bit of a jumble, but I manage to unearth a box of tissues from under a dozen old magazines.

I'm about to push the top drawer shut when I spy three familiar faces peeking out from a photograph. I realize it's a picture of Ava, Nick, and me from an old football game. Nick and I look exhausted but happy, and Ava has both arms around our waists, her smile frozen in time. Her mom must have taken this years ago.

"Barrett?" Her voice prompts me to turn around, and she spies the photo held between my fingers. "Oh, that's a blast from the past. Bring it over."

I do, sitting on the edge of the bed by her feet. She takes the tissues from me with a thank you, then leans over to get a better view of the photograph.

"Oh, dear God. Look at me," she groans.

"What?"

Her eyes widen in surprise. "That was the year I got braces and everyone started calling me bear-trap."

I look down at the photo and chuckle.

Then Ava smiles at me fondly. "You wouldn't let them tease me. You said true beauty was found within."

"I still believe that, you know."

She grins at me. "Is that a nice way of saying I never quite grew into my buck teeth and knobby knees?"

"Not at all. You grew into every part of your body. You're perfection."

The moment the words leave my mouth, I want to stuff them back in but they hang between us. Ava's still watching me, with a curious expression on her face.

"Last night isn't happening again." Getting the words out isn't as easy as I'd like, but I look her right in the eye when I say them. "We can only ever be friends."

I put the picture down between the two of us, and Ava reaches down to touch the edge of it. "Just friends."

"Friends who made a couple of mistakes together. But we're past it," I insist, and reach to put the photograph away, not wanting it to get lost.

Our fingers brush, and even after all these years— and especially after what happened last night—it's that touch that makes me question every single thing in my life. I can feel it bone deep when our eyes meet.

She's perched on the bed beside me, and I lean in without thinking. If she had pulled away, I might have been able to stop, but her mouth meets mine without hesitation. The kiss deepens instantly, full of that hunger we shared last night in the cold.

No one else is here.

No one would know.

Just one more time ... then I'll walk away.

These are the thoughts haunting me as I lean closer to Ava. One of her arms comes around my shoulder to pull me against her. My hands search across the softness of her robe to find the tie in the center, and I'm about to pull it loose when a heavy creak carries up the stairs. The sound is footsteps, and that realization sinks in just as Nick's voice calls out.

"Hey, Ava!" He's still walking up the stairs, getting closer by the second. "Where are you? I have a question."

"Barrett, get..." Ava pushes against my chest. "Get in the closet. Just hide!"

I'm not even sure I can fit in the closet, but her panicked whisper is enough to send me scrambling off the bed and toward the sliding closet door. It rattles a little when I push it open, but I squeeze underneath the rack overhead and yank the door shut a second before I hear Nick walk into the room.

Fuck me. I shouldn't have kissed her, I shouldn't have...

"Nick. What's up?" Her voice has a subtle tremor in it, but not a noticeable one. I hope.

"I was going to bring some coffee back and realized I left my wallet." His knuckles tap against his pocket. "But I saw everything in the kitchen and didn't know where you were. You sick or something?"

"Kind of. I woke up with a cough," Ava says.

"Looks like a fever, too. Your face is all red." Biting back a curse at Nick's words, I pray he doesn't press the issue. "Want me to pick up some meds?"

"That'd be great." Ava sneezes afterwards; at least she doesn't have to fake it. "But for now, I just want to rest."

"Okay, I'll leave you to it." I hear the door creak as Nick steps back out, but then he hesitates. "Have you seen Barrett? Doesn't seem like he's in the house."

"No, but I've been up here for a while, just went down to make myself some tea earlier." Bless her for being able to lie through her teeth. "Maybe he went running or something?"

Nick laughs. "You know, if anyone was going to jog in this terrible weather, it would definitely be Barrett. I'll bring him back some coffee too."

The bedroom door clicks shut, and I finally let out the tense breath I'd been holding. Counting to thirty inside my head, I wait until the last sound from the stairs fade before I chance to step out of the closet. Relief is written all over her face, and my first instinct is to comfort her, but I know better. I have to *do* better.

"We can't be alone together." The words snap out of me, sharp and decisive. "Not in the same room. And it has to be that way until I leave."

My stomach sinks when I see her defeated expression, but I don't give her the chance to answer, walking out of the bedroom before temptation overwhelms me again.

"Feel better," I whisper as I head down the stairs.

Chapter Ten

Ava

"Ah-choo!"

Mom squeezes yet another bottle of lemon juice into whatever concoction she has boiling on the stove and grabs her wooden spoon to stir it. She swears whatever family remedy she's cooking up will have both me and Barrett feeling better by the morning, but I have half a mind to think she's just making hot toddies. Not that I would turn that down, mind you.

"I can't believe both of my best helpers got sick at the same time," she says, throwing a dash of ginger into the pot. "You guys are ruining all the fun."

When she returns to the fridge to dig out her next round of ingredients, I sneak a peek at Barrett. He's slumped over the kitchen table, the tip of his nose cherry red. I shoot him a knowing smile and he lets out a quiet huff before mouthing "your fault," with one eyebrow cocked.

I can't deny that, he's right. Then again, I never would have been out in the cold if he hadn't been all moody and brooding out in his car. And he was the one who kissed me earlier, fully knowing I wasn't feeling well. I guess neither one of us was thinking too much about germs at the time.

I tap the side of my pointer finger against my lips and give him a silent "shush." I try to mouth "keep your tongue to yourself" back at him, but it comes out as more of a whisper.

"What's with the whispering? Do you guys have a secret?" Nick walks into the kitchen and right into the middle of my almost silent conversation with Barrett. I can feel my pulse quickening. Does Nick know? Is he really going to bring this up in front of Mom?

"Did you team up to get me a new car for my birthday?" Nick asks. My heart rate returns to normal. As long as we're dealing with normal, joking Nick, we're in the clear, but the second he's actually suspicious of us, we're done for.

"Yup, you caught us," I admit, hiding my sigh of relief by playing along with the joke. "Any car you want, as long as it's in the twenty-five-dollar range, we'll buy it for you." I punctuate my punch line with another sneeze, which Barrett echoes.

"Whoa, didn't realize I'd wandered into the nurse's office. Keep those sneezes away from me." He backs away swatting away at invisible germs.

"More importantly," Mom interrupts, waving the wooden spoon at Barrett and me, "keep them away from your father. We can't run the risk of him catching anything. I think we're going to have to do some resituating here in terms of sleeping arrangements to keep you two away from the rest of us."

"I can get a hotel," Barrett volunteers, his voice muted with the congestion.

"No, no. Here's what I'm thinking," Mom says, giving the pot another stir. "I think we just keep anyone feeling even the slightest bit feverish on the lower level tonight, everyone else upstairs." She nods to herself, satisfied. "Sick people on one floor, healthy on the other. It's about containment."

"But Moooooooom," I groan, my former whiny teenage-self making a return for a brief stint of complaining. "There's only one pull-out couch down here. Why can't I just sleep in my own bed?"

"And get your father sick right before his big party? I don't think so. I'm sure Nick will be happy to go down to the basement for us and grab the air mattress so you can both sleep in the den." Mom shoots Nick a look through the steam of her bubbling cauldron. "Won't you, Nick?"

"Yeah, sure," Nick says, already shuffling toward the basement door.

"No, Nick, wait!" He jolts to a stop and pivots back to me, startled by the urgency in my voice. I know I sound a little bit too desperate not to spend the night downstairs, but it's almost ten, way past my mother's usual bedtime. I need to come up with a better excuse, and fast.

"Mom, I don't even think I'm sick!" I announce, trying to speak clearly enough to mask my congestion. "It might just be allergies, really. I don't think it's anything worth switching up sleeping arrangements ov-" Just as I've almost finished my monologue, my throat contracts and I break into a coughing fit. Looks like I don't have much of a future in acting.

"Alright, that's enough of that!" Mom instantly grabs the disinfectant spray and waves it through the air, releasing a giant cloud of chemical-laden mist. "Nick, grab the air mattress. Anyone who has blown their nose more than once today, get your germs out of my kitchen. I'll bring you mugs of my remedy when it's done." Frantically waving her hands, she shoos us into the family room. Barrett sinks into one end of the couch and I strategically position myself at the opposite end.

"So much for not being alone together," I mutter under my breath, just loud enough for Barrett to hear. When he turns his head toward me, I can tell that his cheeks are missing a bit of their usual color, and his eyes are drawn with dark circles around them. But God, I didn't think anyone could have flu symptoms and still be that gorgeous.

He's wearing that same pair of sweatpants that I so gracelessly pulled off him in the parking lot just a couple days ago, and there's not much I wouldn't give to reach over and slide them down again. I sink farther into my end of the couch, literally holding myself back.

"Hey, we're both adults," he whispers. "I think we can act like it." The control in his voice insists that he has every intention of behaving, but the flicker in his eyes says just the opposite, and that semi-bulge in his pants, yeah, there's that.

The question is, can I control my emotions *and my libido* spending a night alone with him? I gently bite my lower lip, thinking it over, and Barrett lets out a quiet groan, making no secret of the fact that he's letting his eyes trace my figure, lingering in all his favorite places.

"Stop looking at me like that," I hiss.

"Like what?"

"Like you're gonna strip me naked and take me right here."

The flicker in Barrett's eyes grows to a full-blown flame. Tonight is going to be nothing but bad news.

"Got the mattress!" Nick bursts into the room, with the deflated air mattress.

I leap off my spot on the couch to help get things set up, relieved to escape the sexual tension, at least for now.

Nick and Barrett work on pumping up the mattress while I pull the cushions off the couch, trying to dismiss the innuendo of the term "pull-out bed" from my head.

"I'll grab us some pillows and sheets," I volunteer. No one has to ask me twice to get out of this room for a second.

"No," Nick stops me. "No going upstairs unless you want Mom to unleash another cloud of disinfectant on you. I've got it."

He bounds out of the room and up the stairs, leaving me and Barrett alone again. I don't dare turn around to look at him, trying to focus on lining the couch cushions up in a perfect stack in the corner of the room.

I can feel his eyes on me, but I think I know if I turn around I might pull him onto that air mattress and ride him until we've deflated the thing. Luckily, Nick comes back downstairs, his arms piled high with bedding, before I can entertain the thought for too long. Mom steps in behind him, walking slowly and deliberately to not spill the two mugs of the mystery concoction that she's holding.

"It looks like you guys are gonna be all set down here," she says, surveying our sleeping arrangements. She sets the mugs cautiously down on the end table before backing out of the room, away from our germs. "See?

You'll be just fine. And if you drink all that up while it's still hot, you'll be right as rain tomorrow."

I grab one of the mugs and let the steam warm me. Just smelling it seems to open up my sinuses. Maybe not all of Mom's ideas are quite as bad as this Ava and Barrett slumber party. Three sips later and I'm already feeling like a new woman. "You oughta bottle this stuff, Mom," I say between sips.

"Well, make sure you finish it all before you go to sleep. Which should be soon! We need you all better for the party. C'mon, Nick, let's get out of this petri dish."

Mom and Nick say their good nights from a distance before heading upstairs, but not before Mom makes us swear again to drink all of our tea. Once they're gone and it's just Barrett and me again, my stomach starts fluttering, and it has nothing to do with being sick.

We're alone for an entire night. It's silent for a good long minute. I pick at my cuticles, trying to resist my long-abandoned nail-biting habit. What do we do next? Just go to bed, I guess? How am I supposed to sleep when all I want is for Barrett to keep me up all night? Congestion be damned. Are we really going to sleep in separate beds or…?

"So, I'll take the air mattress?" he finally offers.

Well, that answers that.

"Yeah, if you want, that's fine," I say, dodging his gaze and scrambling to grab a few pillows and blankets from the stack Nick brought down. It looks like Barrett wants to behave after all, which I know is probably the best choice.

I get to work setting up my bed, keeping the conversation to a minimum. Talking has brought us down dangerous roads before, and I'm doing my best to pump the brakes, since I know it's what he wants.

We busy ourselves with gulping down Mom's magic tea and take our respective turns brushing our teeth in the downstairs bathroom, keeping the conversation to the occasional "excuse me" as we pass each other, both of us keeping our hands to ourselves.

Once I see that he's settled onto the air mattress, I hit the lights, stumbling through the darkness till I find the pull-out bed, which squeaks and groans as I climb in.

Alright. Time for sleep. Aaaaaand, do your thing, Sandman. A few minutes pass and still nothing. I've been feeling sick and sleepy all day, why do I have to be wide awake now?

I toss from one side to the other, but it's impossible to get comfortable when I know that temptation himself is lying just a few feet away. I'm not sure how much time passes when Barrett finally whispers into the dark, "Are you sleeping?"

"Not even sort of."

His deep sigh fills the still, silent air. "Jesus, why is this so hard?"

"I don't know, Barrett." His name feels warm on my lips, even warmer than Mom's crazy tea.

"Want to turn on the TV?" he suggests.

I grab my phone from beside the bed and check the time. "No. I usually read before bed," I say.

"In the dark?" he asks, propping himself up on one elbow.

"I read on my phone."

"What do you like to read?"

I smile to myself. "You're going to think it's stupid."

"Try me," he says, voice soft.

I flash him the screen on my phone, it's the latest article I've been reading, and the map of Pangea that had captured my interest for the past two nights.

It's quiet for another second, but then I hear the rustling of him shifting out from underneath his blankets and the light padding of his feet on the carpet.

"May I?" It's almost too dark to see him, but I can feel the pressure of his legs pushed against the side of the bed, waiting for his invitation to climb in.

"Sure," I whisper back. It's against my better judgment, but I slide over to make room for him. The bed bends a bit as he lowers himself onto the springy mattress and slides under the sheets. His body so close to mine but not touching.

"What is it?" He studies the map on my phone for a second before meeting my eyes.

"I love reading about random facts and obscure articles. It relaxes me, I guess. Clears my head. This is about how all the continents on Earth used to be fused together. Did you know that Australia is moving closer to Asia at the rate of two inches per year?"

He reaches out, gently tucking my hair behind my hair with an amused smile. "That's fascinating."

"Don't tease me. You wanted to know the kinds of things I read about."

"I want to know everything about you," he corrects me.

This is such a bad idea.

Chapter Eleven

Barrett

I'm lying on a lumpy pull-out bed with Ava, and I've never wanted to be anywhere more.

I spent the day feeling sick, like I was coming down with the cold she had, but right now, I feel clearheaded and enamored as I listen to her speak. When we're alone, I forget that anything else exists.

"What else do you like to read about?" I ask, watching the way her lips move.

She shrugs, a smile pulling up her mouth. "Everything."

Her eyes change when she talks about weather patterns, and unsolved mysteries, and the secret identity of DB Cooper. I can honestly say she's unlike any girl I've ever met. Maybe it's the head cold, but here in the darkness I feel like I can absorb every detail about her that most people gloss over. The freckle just beneath her left eye. The slope of her upper lip. The way she looks down at her hands when she's explaining something detailed.

Her curiosity about the world is refreshing. She has a huge heart, she cares so damn much. It was always that way.

There are so many things I admire about Ava, the bold way she so plainly states what she wants, the way she goes after her goals, charging them down like a bull to a matador. She's twenty-five years old and jumping in with both feet to run a factory—that says something right there.

We're similar in that way—both of us hungry to prove ourselves, to work hard and succeed at our chosen professions. But even in this, in this taboo flirtation, she has decided that she will succeed. That she must win. And the prize? A certain appendage below my waistband twitches, more than ready to volunteer as tribute, to be conquered and won.

And yeah, maybe that was how this all started that first night she saw me naked—a physical spark that ignited our attraction, but somehow, it would be a lie to say that's all this is. I've admired her for two decades. And to see her again now after so many years is messing with my head, well, both heads, if I'm being honest.

As I listen to her talk about some of Earth's greatest mysteries, I'm drawn back fifteen years.

The memory of her standing on the sidelines at one of my and Nick's football games. She was a high school freshman, and I remember the way she stood there, digging the toe of her tennis shoe into the dirt as she watched a group of teenage guys flirting with the cheerleaders in longing.

The guy she liked that year was a piece of shit, totally not worth her time, but you'd be blind to miss the way she looked at him.

I pulled off my helmet, and jogged over to where she stood when coach called a timeout.

"Hey," I said, tilting her chin toward mine.

Her braces glinted under the bright lights, and she smiled up at me.

"Things won't always be this way."

She blinked, either not understanding, or not accepting my meaning. "What?"

"You're too good for him." I nodded to the idiot boys staring at the cheerleaders' boobs.

After looking his way, she swallowed, and her eyes swung back over and met mine.

"Are you feeling better?" she asks, breaking me from my daydream.

I take a deep breath to clear my head. "Strangely, yeah. I think that concoction your mom made us drink actually worked."

She nods, agreeing, then bites her lower lip. "Can we just lie together for a little while?"

"Come here," I roll closer, and open my arms.

She scoots closer and the warmth of her curves against the firm planes of my body is immediately too much.

Being near her after all these years, and seeing the woman she's grown into? It'd be impossible not to want her.

My cock begins to harden and grow, and though I've promised myself a thousand times nothing will happen I find myself wanting to play *just the tip*. Fuck, it'd probably be all she could handle anyway. When she rode my fingers to orgasm in my car, I felt how deliciously tight she was.

The way she squeezed and clenched around me almost made me come untouched.

And now I'm fully hard. That's super helpful.

A shift of her hips closer lets me know she felt it, and how could she not? It's like someone wedged a two by four between us.

She reaches back, pushing her fingers into the hair at the back of my neck, and lightly caresses me as we lie together. It feels so good, and so right, I don't have it in me to tell her to stop.

I know right then this won't be easy. It's in this exact moment I know I've already fallen for her, and that I probably won't ever get over my big, messy, fucked-up feelings for her.

She can't be mine.

Can't.

Because I'll never be able to give her the time she deserves on top of all the other things that stand in our way. So why am I torturing myself?

Because the thought of not touching her is a fate worse than death.

Chapter Twelve

Ava

My frame fits perfectly against Barrett's, like two interlocking puzzle pieces that finally snapped together. His breath is hot against my ear and the scruff of his cheek grazes my neck, making every inch of my skin tingle. He sweeps my hair to the side and kisses me behind my ear and down my neck, his hand wrapped snugly against my hip as he slowly starts grinding his pelvis against me. I let out a little whimper, but he softly lets out a soft "Shh."

He's right. We may be on a different floor, but we're still under my parents' roof. My heart is about to beat out of my chest, and my hands are trembling. God, it feels like high school, trying to make out without my parents catching us. Why does that turn me on?

Barrett turns me over so that we're facing each other. After an entire day spent trying to avoid him, having him here, so close, it's impossible to resist.

"Sorry I got you sick," I murmur.

"It was worth it," he whispers back.

I smile at him and watch as his features transform and he breaks into a chuckle. "What?"

"I was just remembering that time you were sick with the stomach flu."

"Which time?" Thankfully it hasn't happened often, but I don't know what he's referring to.

"I was fourteen, so you must have been, what? Nine?"

Sometimes I forget about our age difference. I nod. "Yeah, I remember that. It was awful."

"You were so funny back then. You couldn't remember that it was called a stomach bug so you kept telling everyone you had a stomach beetle."

I swat his arm. "Shush."

The number of embarrassing stories Barrett knows about me could fill an entire evening.

"I thought it was cute," he says, touching my cheek.

His lips touch tentatively against mine for the briefest, sweetest of kisses.

The soft thud of footsteps on the stairs makes both of us lock up, frozen in position. It suddenly feels like the time for prayer. *Dear God, whoever it is, please don't let them turn on the lights.*

The steps get closer, padding past us and into the kitchen. My hands quiver in their white-knuckle grip on Barrett's t-shirt. What would we say if we got caught? That the air mattress was uncomfortable? That sleep kissing is totally just as common as sleepwalking?

Neither of us so much as breathes as we listen to whoever is in the kitchen get a glass from the cabinet and turn the faucet on, then off again. We wait for the clunk of the glass being set in the sink, then the padding of the feet heading back up the stairs again.

We take a deep breath in perfect unison. I can hardly hold back my giggles as Barrett gets back to working over my neck with his mouth.

"Why does this have to feel so good when I know it's so, so wrong?"

He chuckles softly, lifting himself onto one elbow so he can look down at me. "You still feel sick?" he asks.

I shake my head. "No. Not really. Just incredibly turned on."

I don't know what it is about him that loosens my inhibitions. Maybe it's because I've known him so many years, but he makes me feel comfortable, and safe, like I can really be myself.

He groans and leans down to kiss me again, more deeply this time, his tongue tangling exquisitely with mine.

I shift restlessly beside him, wanting more contact, but knowing I'm probably not going to get it.

But then he surprises me by tossing back the sheets and laying his hand flat against my belly—low, like almost touching my panties. His expression is pained, like he's fighting with himself.

"Promise you can stay quiet?"

I nod, barely breathing.

"Then let me take care of it."

He shifts down to a kneeling position on the floor. Oh fuck, he's not going to…is he? Grabbing my ankles, he pulls me toward him so that my legs are hanging off the end of the bed and his face is right between my legs. Fuck, he totally is.

It's Barrett's turn to pull *my* sweatpants down, but this time, there's nothing even slightly accidental about it. With two swift fingers, he pulls my panties to the side and runs a teasing tongue right through me, making my stomach twist in delight.

After several more teasing licks, he takes the waistband of my panties in his teeth and tugs them to the floor. Fuck, he's smooth. I kick my panties off into the darkness and Barrett pushes my knees apart, studying me with a dark, lust-filled gaze that makes my belly flip.

"You are exquisite. You're literally perfect," he says, eyes studying my flesh as he runs one long finger along my core. "You know that, don't you?"

I don't have words as his finger caresses me in light, teasing circles, so instead I make a wordless whimper of approval.

"You like that?" he asks. His voice sounds reverent, and his gaze follows the movement of his finger, sweeping over my slick flesh.

I nod, eyes on his. He is so handsome it physically pains me to look at him sometimes. His t-shirt pulls at the chiseled muscles of his chest, and there's dark hair on his jaw, but it's his eyes that always get me—the way they seem to see straight inside of me.

"Come here." I groan out a frustrated noise, reaching one hand along his chest, down to his abs. "You never let me touch you."

"Not necessary. Touching you is everything. Trust me."

And then there are no more words because he lowers his mouth again, and begins tasting me in slow, hot kisses that I'm pretty sure will drive me completely insane.

I make a wordless sound of need-filled pleasure as Barrett kisses my wet, swollen flesh again, picking up the tempo. Everything ratchets up six-thousand degrees, and I can't help but push my hands into his hair.

"You taste delicious," he says, voice tight.

"Don't you dare stop," I moan as his warm mouth latches onto my pussy like it's his freaking job.

"Wasn't planning on it."

Barrett *Fucking* Wilson—my older brother's best friend, and my own personal walking wet-dream for the past decade—is sucking on my lady-bits. I let out a sharp groan.

"Shh." He lifts his face from the spot between my legs and places a finger over his lips. "Be quiet or they'll hear you."

I glance down the hall—we're supposed to be sleeping in the den tonight, not making it our own personal love shack. It should bother me that my parents are under the same roof, it should prevent me from becoming oh-my-God-so-horny, but with Barrett kneeling on the carpet at my feet, head between my thighs as he brings me to heights of pleasure I could never imagine in even my wildest dreams about him, that doesn't even factor into the equation.

Why does the fact that this is forbidden and we could be discovered at any moment make me even hotter?

I gaze down at him, tangling my hands in his hair. His strong jaw, with dark stubble moves as he kisses me intimately. He parts me with his fingers, his tongue doing the most magical things.

He is like a Jedi-ninja of pussy eating. I could watch him do this all day. And somehow, I know I'm going to remember him doing this for the rest of my life.

Ever since I'd accidentally walked in on him in the shower our first night here, I'd been done for. I'd seen what he was packing in his jeans and mama wanted to play. He'd been out of reach my entire life, but now I was more than old enough to go after what I wanted.

"More," I beg, already so close.

"I'm going to fuck you with my fingers."

"God, yes," I say on a desperate sob. Why is he telling me this? Almost like he's asking permission. After the past three days of banter, and flirting and arguing, I thought it'd be pretty obvious that I wanted this. Wanted him.

While continuing to work me over with his mouth, Barrett sinks one thick finger inside me, groaning as he finds me soaked.

Fuckity, fuck. This is so good.

"I want you."

He shakes his head, that cocky smirk I've always loved crossing his lips. "You can't handle me and we both know it."

He's probably right, but I'd never backed down from a challenge, and riding the biggest cock I'd ever seen sounds like a fun way to test my limits.

"But don't you want me to…?"

"Can't. Bro code," he manages in between licks of his tongue against me.

Screw bro code. His face was already between my thighs. And yes, he was besties with my brother, but surely making me come on his face is also against this supposed law of bros.

"Hmm. So blue balls for you then?" I pant, blood pumping through my veins faster and faster.

He moans, tongue tracing lazy circles against me, like he could do this all day. "I have hands. I'll take care of it later."

God, he is so infuriating with his boundaries and rules and control. Is it bad that I would literally pay good money to watch him jack off that beast of a cock? I could imagine myself sitting there, slack-jawed with a tub of buttered popcorn in lap. And yes, the popcorn would be buttered, this is my fantasy after all.

"Can I watch you *take care of it*?" I ask, knowing what he'll probably say. And get a moan in response from him.

That visual caused a reaction because his movements begin to ramp up. The idea of me watching him excites him...

After a few more seconds, Barrett groans again, almost like he's in agony. "You going to come for me, sweetheart?"

"Gladly."

My back bridges up as Barrett's tongue teases against me just right, his fingers reaching to the softest spot deep within me to pull what he wants out from me—a whimper, a gasp, and a mind-blowingly perfect orgasm. My spine collapses against the mattress in a jolt as I pant desperately, trying to find my breath again.

"Good girl."

He half kisses, half bites my inner thigh and my whole body contracts. I can feel his mouth curve into a smirk on my skin before he hoists himself back up onto the bed.

I think he may have zapped the last of whatever energy this cold hasn't taken out of me. But how can I not return the favor? Maybe I can get him to set aside that all-powerful bro code for just one night.

Once he's back on the bed, I pull myself tight against him, but that alone takes all the strength I have left. There's no way I could do him any justice with how drained I am. My kisses are slow and sleepy with long breaths in between. Fuck.

I grab at the waistband of his sweatpants, but instead of pawing at that beautiful cock that stands at attention for me, I can only steady myself against his hips for a second before sinking into the bed. Damn, I'm beat.

Luckily, Barrett doesn't seem to mind. He chuckles a bit, folding me tightly into his arms. "Go to sleep, Ava," he whispers, placing a final kiss on my cheek. My heavy eyelids flutter closed. He doesn't have to tell me twice.

Chapter Thirteen

Barrett

I wake up to the warm scent of Ava's hair filling my senses, and her body pressed right against mine.

I hadn't meant to fall asleep like this, holding her wrapped in my arms. My cock certainly approves, though, pressed right against the soft curve of her ass.

I think back to last night, talking, and then pleasuring her with my mouth.

Hot blood courses through my veins, and fuck, suddenly I have never wanted something more.

How I'm supposed to untangle myself from her when every inch of me is hard and ready?

The fact is, I don't want to. Just because we can't sleep together doesn't mean I can't have another taste of what I want, and watching Ava's face light up in orgasmic bliss is so damn satisfying. Nudging her thigh with my knee, I part her legs just enough for my hand to slide along her thigh. She makes a small murmur of approval in her sleep, and my heart riots in my chest.

Pushing my hand past the waistband of her pajama pants, I find her underwear is still damp from the night before, and that fills me with a hot sort of pride, remembering how she was practically grinding against my tongue for more. She is so damn sexy.

I'd love to have her in my mouth again, but it's early enough that people will start waking up, and there's no darkness to hide us now. My fingers draw slow strokes up and down her panties, adding a bit more pressure until a soft gasp escapes her lips. Sleep-dazed eyes open to meet mine, desire written all over her face when she realizes what I'm doing to her.

"Barrett," she moans my name low and ragged, the sound hitting me straight in the groin.

Fuuuck.

"We have to keep quiet," I whisper back, leaning down to seal her lips with a kiss.

I slip under her panties to the slick skin beneath. She's so wet, heat spreading onto my fingers with every touch, and I have to be inside her one way or another. Ava muffles another noise against my lips as my finger thrusts deep, sinking all the way to the knuckle. I can't believe how tight she is around me, and despite the constant temptation, I'm really not sure if she could handle me. I can't stop thinking about her trying, though.

The look of hot determination that I'm sure would be painted across her face, the rosy blush creeping up her neck, the throaty whimpers she'd make as I sank myself all the way into her snug warmth…

Pre-come leaks from my dick, and I have to take a deep breath to calm the fuck down. I feel like a teenager again, out of control and desperate.

Ava's hips jerk forward when I ease in a second finger in beside the first, my thumb circling in a firm, deliberate rhythm. I know we don't have time, I know how much of a risk this is, but when she turns toward me, and grasps my shoulders to keep me close, her lips find mine, and it's impossible to pull away.

"You like sneaking around like this, don't you?" She shivers at my question, and I smile as the next thrust makes her delicate inner muscles squeeze tight around my fingers. "Answer me, Ava."

"Yes, God, yes." She's rocking into every movement of my hand now, and every time her thigh brushes against my cock, it takes every ounce of self-control I have not to pin her down and work my shaft inside that tight, clinging heat.

"Do you want to come for me again?" I whisper against her parted lips. It was so good when she gave in against my tongue, and I need to feel that one more time. Then I'll get a handle on myself, I'll just jerk off and put her out of my mind...

"Barrett, fuck." Ava orgasms around my fingers seconds after her desperate curse, gripping my shoulders almost tight enough to bruise. I stay with her until the aftershocks of pleasure fade, her clit swollen and sensitive when I tease it again.

I'm going to explode in my boxers if I don't get up and do something about my own needs, but still I find I can't get up and leave just yet.

Pulling my hand from her panties, I bring my fingers to my mouth and suck them clean.

Her eyes widen, watching me, and I know instantly it was the wrong move. She's so fucking sexy and she tastes so good—sweet and feminine and completely aroused.

Knowing that I was the one who did that to her does something to me. Something primal and animalistic.

"I...I've got to go clean up," I mutter, throwing off the blankets.

A seductive light spills into Ava's eyes, and both hands leave my shoulders, caressing down my chest and starting to go lower. "I could clean you up."

The only way I can refuse is by looking straight up at the ceiling, knowing Nick is right up there. I blow out a slow, tortuous exhale. He'd kill me for going this far, much less letting his sister give me a handjob in their den.

"Code still applies," I add under my breath, and Ava sighs before letting me go. She might think I'm stubborn, but it's critical that at least one of us is trying to keep us safe.

I manage to sneak to the bathroom to wash my hands, but a brief glance in the mirror is enough to prove the tent in my pants isn't going away. Unable to hold back any longer, I push my pants down to mid-thigh and start working myself in quick strokes, one hand braced against the counter. My cock is so hot and stiff in my palm, I know I won't last long.

Each time my eyes fall closed, all I can think of is Ava so mercifully tight around my fingers, and what it would be like if I could really have her. And not just her body, but *her*, all of her.

A quick orgasm makes another mess of my hands, but at least my cock starts to back down while I wash up one more time. The logical thing to do would be to go back to bed—my bed—and stay away from Ava, but it's crazy how drawn I am to her.

I don't remember the last time a woman made me feel this way. If it was just sex, this would be cut and dry, but it's not. There's her family, there's my entire life hanging in the balance. Ava isn't some one-night hook-up I'm happy to see leave once the deed is done.

Shaking my head, I decide to go down to the kitchen and make some coffee. If I'm going to be awake, I might as well get my day going.

The coffee begins dripping into the carafe when I hear distant footsteps, and I'm bracing myself to see Ava again when Nick walks into the kitchen, yawning and stretching his arms up over his head. It's a damn good thing I didn't call to her by name and say something very inappropriate.

"What are you doing up so early?" I ask, trying to keep my tone casual.

"Slept weird. Decided to give up on trying." Nick spies the coffee in progress and looks deeply relieved. "You feeling better, man?"

I am, actually, and that's a surprise. "Way better."

"Must have just been a one-day bug or something," he declares, leaning against the counter while waiting for the water to filter through.

I nod, and it's the hardest thing in the world not to be honest with him. Nick is my best friend, without question, and if he had come down twenty minutes earlier, he might have seen me with my hand in his sister's panties. I don't know how I'd justify it to him, even if some part of me wants to, knowing how I feel about her.

"You went over to your mom's the other night, right?" Nick asks, snapping me out of that train of thought. "Things still pretty rough?"

"Yeah." There wasn't any point in lying about it; he's known about the situation with my mom. "It really is a full house."

I was the oops baby, the teenage pregnancy she was never proud of, and I felt every bit of that growing up. It's one of the reasons I always insisted on a condom. I never wanted to put a child in the situation I grew up in—feeling unwanted and unloved.

He gives my shoulder a friendly smack, his smile wide. "Hey, you're family here and always will be. Don't let that get you down when you've got so many amazing things in your life."

Nick's right, and because he's right, I can't tell him the truth. After his divorce and everything else, the last thing he needs is finding out Ava and I nearly hooked up. I've just got to man up and get over her.

I'll be gone after the party tomorrow. One more day and we can pretend this never happened.

* * *

"Love is a sham," Nick says, taking a sip of his beer. "I get now why you're so anti-commitment."

We're seated at the bar of a local restaurant, where we came to grab some burgers and catch up. Nick's been uncharacteristically quiet about his split from Vanessa, but I have a feeling that's about to change.

"I'm not anti-commitment, for the record," I say, pushing away my plate, suddenly no longer hungry.

At this, he laughs. "Bullshit. You have a different girl in your bed every weekend."

That may have been the old Barrett, the horny college kid enjoying his freedom for the first time, but honestly that's not me anymore. It hasn't been for a long time, but it's interesting to know that's how he still sees me. Yes, I like to blow off steam, and yes I love sex, but I'm not a player by any means. It's more than not having the time at this point. It just doesn't interest me anymore.

I shrug. "I usually work at least eighty hours a week, I just don't have time for a relationship right now, but that doesn't mean I don't want one someday."

Nick shakes his head, swallowing the last bite of his burger. "Take it from me, man. Avoid that shit like the plague." He nods to my fries. "Are you going to finish those?"

I shake my head. "Have at it."

"Thanks." He grabs a handful and drops them on his plate.

He eats in silence for a few minutes, looking lost in thought.

"You want to talk about what happened?" I ask. I don't want to push him, I just want him to know I'm here in case he does. This is an integral part of the bro code, being there for your best friend when he goes through something tough. Even if it's just to listen and agree with whatever shit went down with the opposite sex. Whether you agree with it or not.

Nick exhales and pushes his plate away. He's silent for a few seconds, his brows pushed together. "She cheated," he finally says.

"Shit. That sucks. I'm sorry, man," I say.

He shrugs. "Found out right after the wedding that she slept with her ex-boyfriend right before we got married."

I press my lips together. Nick had only been dating Vanessa a couple of months when they hopped on a plane to Vegas and got hitched, surprising everyone. It wasn't my place to point out that a spur-of-the moment wedding at a drive-thru chapel may not be the foundation that would result in lasting love. "How are you doing? Really?"

He takes a long sip of his beer. "Better, actually. My plan now is to take a page from your playbook and just enjoy the single life."

I grit my teeth. I know this image he has of me—the always single, never tied down, never commit, never be seen with the same woman twice persona—is not going to serve me well if I ever do grow a pair and admit how I feel about his sister.

Hello rock, meet hard place.

I take a long drink of my beer, lost in thought, before I realize Nick is still talking.

The word Ava snaps me out of my distraction.

"...you know? I'm glad she's single. I mean, my parents pressure her, but with everything she has going on I think it's for the best. Plus, if someone ever hurt her I'd kill the motherfucker."

The food in my stomach feel like battery acid, and I shakily nod my agreement. "Absolutely."

Chapter Fourteen

Barrett

I get my suit in order while everyone else is busy getting everything ready at the hotel for the retirement party tonight. The hotel I should have stayed at in the next town over instead of the Saunders' place. They're expecting at least a hundred people, and I want to show Mr. Saunders the respect he deserves by showing up right on time.

Ava and I barely glimpsed each other this morning. She was on her way out to start the logistics of putting together all the pieces of the party, and with the house to myself, I feel a lot more level-headed.

The same way I prep for a big deal, I can set myself up for what will happen tonight. Small talk, drinks, and a toast in my suit pocket to memorize before everyone makes the rounds. I'm in my element.

That's what I remind myself as I walk into the hotel, checking my cufflinks and the crisp lines of my jacket. I follow the sign pointing to the banquet hall, mentally running through my agenda; find my seat, grab some champagne, before shaking a whole lot of hands.

Then I glimpse Ava across the room.

She's in a black dress that I've never seen before. It clings to every curve of her body, the neckline darting low enough to be enticing but still high enough to be considered decent. My thoughts are anything but decent as my gaze travels lower, to how the fabric drapes around her hips, cutting off right at the knee. Stockings frame her calves the rest of the way down to a pair of matching heels, and I have to steady myself before meeting her eyes.

When her gaze meets mine, I suddenly forget about the makeup and the jewelry, the way her hair is pulled back to show off her beautiful heart-shaped face. It's dangerous to hold her gaze, for us to visually flirt with this kind of risk while everyone else is in the room. But inconveniently, it's the only thing I want to do.

Knowing I need to resist temptation I break away first, turning to go find the champagne. This won't work if I don't keep my distance. Focusing on the party is the priority. Then I'll go into my own room, sleep, and leave tomorrow. That's all that has to happen. That's all that can happen.

The night slowly melts away, my toast to Mr. Saunders delivered flawlessly, an amazing dinner and a celebratory cake eventually fading into chatter around the tables. I check the time, realizing it's late enough to politely excuse myself, and say one last goodbye to Ava's parent's before ducking out into the hall.

As I approach her parents, Ava's mom opens her arms for a hug. I smile, and return her embrace.

"I'm so glad that you came, Barrett. It really means a lot." Her eyes are misty, and she blinks the tears away before allowing herself to get too emotional.

I reach out and shake hands with Mr. Saunders. "When Nick invited me, I didn't want to miss it. I don't get back into town very often anymore, but you guys are like a second family to me."

Ava's dad smiles warmly, pumping my hand twice more before releasing it. "We're damn proud of you, son. I know it's not easy for you, and I just—" he pauses, pressing his lips together to compose himself. "You've grown into a great young man."

"Thank you." His words hit me straight in the chest, and stay lodged there. I never really felt like I had a father at all. Nick's dad was the closest thing I really had. He was the one who taught me how to ride my bike, and how to throw a spiral. Suddenly I feel like even more of an asshole for lusting after his daughter.

"Are you driving back in the morning?" Mrs. Saunders asks.

I nod. "Yeah. I think I'm actually going to go upstairs and get some sleep."

"Drive safely tomorrow."

We share another hug, and another handshake, and then I'm heading out of the reception hall.

Pressing the button for an elevator, I'm congratulating myself on a plan well executed when the doors slide open.

Ava is standing alone in the car, and I can't hide my surprise. She's so gorgeous, I have to physically steady myself. Stuffing my hands in my pockets is the only thing that stops me from reaching out for her. It's maddening how tempting she looks tonight. All those curves hidden behind a silky black dress, matching heels, dark hair twisted into an elegant knot at the nape of her neck to show off those delicate collarbones that I've fantasized about nibbling on.

"What are you—"

"Mom thought she left Dad's present upstairs, then texted me and said she found it." Ava laughs but doesn't step out of the elevator. "Going up?" Her blue eyes dance mischievously on mine.

"Yeah." *I was going to, anyway.* "Aren't you getting out?"

I move to catch the doors before they slide shut, and that step forward is enough for a fire to light up Ava's eyes. The answer to my question is revealed in her gaze as she looks me up and down. She wants me and isn't even trying to hide it, which instantly ups the ante on this cat-and-mouse game we've been playing all weekend.

"Aren't you coming in?" she asks, her voice low and sultry.

No one else is in the hall. No one would know she and I had ever crossed paths, much less that we ended up in the same elevator. And tonight is it, my final night in town, a thought that's been bothering me all day.

Unable to say no to her, I step into the elevator and the doors slide shut behind me.

It was just one step, but the meaning behind it is huge. Monumental.

The moment we're alone, really alone, she steps forward to place one hand on my jaw and rises on tiptoe. Her lips are inches from mine and her soft feminine scent is enough to send my heart into overdrive.

Ava wets her lower lip and leans in close. It isn't a choice—it's raw instinct—when I lean down and take her mouth with a deep, searing kiss. The kiss I'd been trying not to lay on her since I first saw her all dressed up. The heat that's been building in my body the entire night threatens to combust, and a groan catches in my throat when she puts one hand over my crotch, pressing her palm against my heat. I harden instantly at her forbidden touch. I've been following the bro code this entire week, hell, for over a decade, and that one touch obliterated every rule I've hidden behind.

Fuck.

Feeling the warmth of her palm against me—when it's what I've wanted for years—is torture. But before I can remove her hand, she leans in closer.

"I want this tonight," she whispers against my mouth, and the light squeeze that follows sends a jolt through my entire body. "I want all of you."

Screw crossing the line. The line is a faint and distant memory. All I want is to hear Ava say that again, preferably as I'm sliding inside of her.

With my hands on her waist, I take two steps forward until her back presses against the wall of the elevator, and my lips crash down on hers. She whimpers and presses her hips against mine, a slow grind of her pelvis causing my knees to tremble.

"Think you can handle it?" I ask, nipping her bottom lip between my teeth and grinding my now fully erect cock against her. "It's not nice to tease a man."

She looks up at me helplessly and makes a wordless whimper. "I'd give anything to try," she says, finding her voice.

Jesus.

Why is that so sexy?

I'm forcing a deep inhale into my lungs, fighting to get myself under control, when the cool plastic of Ava's room key fits into my hand as she slides it between my fingers.

Pulling away just enough to fix the slight smudge of her lipstick, she says, "Come find me later," then presses the button to open the doors again and slips down the hall toward the party.

Turning the key over in my hand, I check the room number, and adjust my cock to keep myself presentable before tapping the button for the next floor. I have to get myself under control—and fast—before I make a mistake so huge, there will be no coming back.

* * *

I wait until everyone else should be asleep.

The key slides through perfectly, and the moment the lock clicks I slip inside. It's dim inside, just the soft glow of a single lamp to light the room. Lust already has me half-crazed, but all logical thought evaporates when I see Ava on her bed in that dress. She smiles, and I don't even have to say what I'm here for—she knows.

Because I'm addicted and so is she. Helpless to the idea of feeling her skin against mine.

We meet in the middle of the room for another deep kiss. I'm so hungry for her, like there's a need in my body that only she can satisfy. I walk Ava back against the bed while her fingers unbutton my suit jacket and grip her from behind, lifting her up and onto the mattress.

"I meant it, Barrett." Ava moans into our next kiss as I strip off my jacket, her hands working my shirt open, button by button, "I want all of you tonight."

"You'll have to work for it," I pant back, finding where her dress unzips and pulling down until the fabric is pooled around her hips.

"That's true with everything good, isn't it?" she quips, letting out a breathy gasp as I kiss down the line of her jaw, past her collarbone to the swell of her breasts.

My teeth scrape over smooth skin as I catch one of the straps of her bra, tugging it loose and down one shoulder. I don't even have the patience to find the clasp, because I simply need more bare skin, more of her. I use my hands to yank the tangled sheath of Ava's dress down her hips, letting it fall to her ankles before she kicks it away, losing a heel in the process.

I focus on her breasts, teasing both hard nipples with my lips and tongue while she shivers against me, hands fumbling to work open the buckle of my belt. It takes another firm tug to get my pants past the bulge of my cock but I deny Ava the chance to free it from my boxers by sinking down to my knees in front of her.

"Barrett, I swear to God…" she starts.

"If you want it, this comes first," I insist, pushing my fingers underneath the lace band of her panties.

Pushing them aside bares her to me, and I kiss her there lightly before burying my face between her thighs. She gasps sharply, one hand shifting to grasp my hair, and I don't stop licking and sucking until she's writhing and trembling against my mouth.

The next time she moans my name, I look up to meet her eyes, needing to see exactly what I'm doing to her, and Ava tugs me up toward her for a kiss.

I rise to my feet, and as we kiss, hot pulls of her tongue against mine, one of her hands explores my abs and the other pushes down my boxers.

She breaks the kiss just long enough to look at me, desperate desire burning in her gaze as she sees me hard and ready.

For a moment, she just stares, taking me all in, and I swear I feel her gaze like an actual caress, all the way from the tip of my sensitive head down to my balls.

"Don't hold back," she demands, "not this time."

If I was going to hold back, I never would have come up to her room. I would have never let her touch me. The moment I feel her small hand curl around my shaft, I'm done for.

She gives an experimental stroke, testing the weight of me in her hand.

I swallow and look down to where she cradles me.

Fuck.

Wrong move.

It's so erotic, the sight of me getting worked over by Ava—fuckin' Ava, every off-limit, forbidden and taboo fantasy I've ever had. It's happening right now.

"Use both hands," I say, the words like gravel in my throat.

She licks her lips, determined, and starts stroking me in firmer strokes now, using both hands.

Having her hands on me is even better than I ever imagined. I could die a happy man right now. But the night's not over, not by a long shot.

Chapter Fifteen

Ava

"Ava—" Barrett groans, his hands pushing into his hair as my palm slides up and along the full, glorious length of him.

I press my other hand against his chest, and silence him with a deep kiss that holds everything I feel for him.

Trust.

Admiration.

Respect.

His hand slides around my ass and tightens, his fingers digging into my flesh. My heartbeat is hot and fast, pumping out a frenzied rhythm.

I didn't even know it could *be* like this.

Before I can lose my bravado, I angle my head near his ear and murmur, "I'm tired of your hands-off rule. Will you let me return the favor?"

"What do you want, Ava?" His eyes meet mine. "Let me hear you say it."

The rough growl of his voice makes me shiver.

"You. In my mouth."

"Fuck." He kisses me hard and lets his hands trail over the swell of my hip, around the curve of my breast, and up to tangle in my hair.

I kiss his neck, nip at the vein where his pulse races as fast as mine, and then my knees hit the carpet. If you'd asked me a month ago whether I'd get excited about going down on a guy, I'd have rolled my eyes and said bitch, please. But right now, I can't think of anything I want more.

I run my palms over his hard thighs and press my lips to the vee of muscle that points toward the main event.

His dick twitches and I lick my lips. Starting at the base, I give soft, sucking nibbles up the silky hard shaft. Encouraged by his ragged breathing, I grip him and flick my tongue along the taut skin. I smile as he throbs, swelling even larger.

He groans my name when I finally take him in my mouth.

All weekend he'd amazed me with his self-control, pleasuring me and taking none for himself. It'd been maddening. But I get it now. Watching someone else come undone is really freaking hot.

I tighten my grip and take as much of him as I can handle, painstakingly slow. I concentrate on the little sounds, the changes in his breathing.

His hand tightens in my hair and heat spreads between my legs.

Barrett gives a half-suppressed moan, and I glance up, expecting to see him watching me. But his head is turned, his mouth hanging slightly open and his chest is heaving. I draw back and follow his gaze. His stormy blue eyes meet mine in the full-length mirror across the room.

I start moving my hand again, watching his face intently. Barrett's eyes flicker downward. It's safe to say I've never seen myself the way I look right now. A handful of enormous, man-god, lips swollen, cheeks pink, hair a mess, and ass bare in a lacy thong. Still holding his gaze, I cup my breast, squeezing one pink nipple between two fingers.

He moans again. "Dammit, Ava. If you keep doing that, I'll—"

With a wicked grin, I slide my free hand down my stomach and under the lace.

Whatever he was about to say evaporates. My hand and mouth work together, a slow glide at first and then faster. Every sound he makes turns me on more. My tongue flicks over the tip before I suck him in again.

"Baby. Gonna come…" His voice is so tight, it sends tingles shooting straight down my spine, causing every muscle south of my bellybutton to clench down—hard.

He strokes my cheek, watching me with wonder. "Where do you want it?"

I don't answer, but I'm ready when he tries to pull my head away, and as his hips buck forward, I keep my mouth sealed around him, and hold him there until his spasms finish.

"Oh, God, Ava. I'm so sorry, I didn't mean to . . . fuck."

I swallow and giggle, and he hauls me up for a quick kiss.

"Get ready," he says.

"For what? Oh!"

He scoops my legs out from under me, strides to the bed, and tosses me on its pillowy surface.

"For everything I can think of."

Chapter Sixteen

Barrett

I join Ava on the bed, and we lie side by side, our heads close, resting on the same pillow and our lips almost touching. I can't help my hands from exploring right now. For once we're not in a car, or her parents' den, where there was no time to linger. Her breasts are soft and warm in my hands, and when I stroke between her thighs, I find her soaking wet.

She begins her slow torture again, jacking me up and down in steady motions. I could let her do this all night, watching the gentle sway of her breasts as she works, feeling the pleasure shoot straight through my spine, pooling low.

"You sure you're ready?" I ask.

She nods, her lips brushing mine. "I couldn't live the rest of my life without knowing how you felt. How you move."

Pleasure snaps through me, and I take another deep breath.

I feel the exact same way. Except forget living the rest of my life, I can't live one more heartbeat without feeling her.

"I have condoms," she says, halting her motions. "In my purse…"

I give my head a gentle shake. "They won't fit."

A blessing or a curse, but I have to special order my condoms from a website that sells size XXL. Ava, of course wouldn't have known that. Rising from the bed, I find my pants and pull out a couple of condoms from my pocket, tossing them onto the bed. Even in the dimly lit room, the black foil wrappers stand in stark contrast to the white duvet.

She rises up on her knees, her eyes dark with lust as she watches me tear open a foil packet with my teeth and draw out the condom, wrestling it onto my hard-on with ease.

I rejoin her on the bed, in our previous position, side by side. I've thought about this moment, way more than I probably should have, and determined this would be the best position for us. In missionary, I could thrust too deep, and in girl-on-top she could impale herself too far down on my shaft, bruising her deep inside. The last thing I want to do is hurt her.

Her eyes are on mine, and she's biting her lip, looking more vulnerable than ever.

"You have no idea how badly I've wanted this," I admit, gritting my teeth as I watch her stroke her fingernails along the ridges and dips in my defined abs.

Placing my hand against the back of her knee, I lift her thigh, opening her, and place it over my hip.

Fitting the head of my cock to her entrance is enough to unravel another thread of self-control. But rather than bury myself balls-deep in her tight heat, I guide myself back and forth, rubbing against her slick heat, and earning me more of those pleasure-filled whimpers that I love.

"Are you sure about this?" I ask.

Ava rolls her eyes playfully. "Don't make me slap you."

With the first slow push forward, I can feel how unbelievably tight she is, and have to suck in a hard breath between my teeth. She needs time to relax around me, even if neither of us wants to wait.

"Still with me?" I whisper, fighting for control.

"You feel even bigger than you look," she confesses with a soft whimper, spreading her legs even wider to welcome me in.

"I promise I'll take care of you," I whisper, sinking inside inch by desperately slow inch. "I'll make it feel so good, Ava."

Words escape her for a moment, and she answers with a nod, nails biting into my abs while I ease into that hot, unrelenting tightness. She feels perfect, but it's not until I'm settled completely inside her that I even think of moving. I kiss her, again and again, and slowly roll my hips, wanting her to feel exactly how deep I am now.

"Barrett..." she says my name in the sexiest, throatiest growl I've ever heard her make.

How am I supposed to think when she whispers my name like a prayer?

"You'll tell me if it hurts?" I groan, feeling delirious and drunk on her already.

Her head gives a tight nod. She looks like she's concentrating. On accepting me, I'd guess.

Bringing one hand between us, I place my thumb on her slick clit, rubbing it in gentle circles as my cock stays buried deep inside the tightest, sweetest heat I've ever felt.

She groans, and her body bucks toward mine.

"If it hurts, I'll tell you. But I need, I have to feel you move..."

I start out with an even rhythm, controlled and deliberate despite every instinct inside me clamoring for more, and Ava's answering moan is a symphony to my ears. Her hands slide up to my pecs, framing the muscles there, and cling tight against my skin as I build the pace. My eyes stay locked on hers between kisses, watching for any sign of discomfort, but all I see is a quickening ecstasy, one that makes me pulse with need.

I've never felt anything better in all my life, and in an instant, I know she's immediately ruined me for other women. Because everything about her is different from her mind, to her humor, to the way she touches me. Despite the need to come, I want to make this good for her, so I fuck her like that for a long time, stroking her inner walls in a deliberate rhythm, again and again.

It's perfection.

"I'm going to come soon," I admit, even though I don't want her to know she's shattered my stamina.

"Faster," Ava gasps against my mouth, "I'm getting close."

I can feel it with every wave of tightness around my shaft, but she's so wet now that I'm hellbent on giving her exactly what she wants. Capturing her mouth in another deep kiss, I work my hand between our bodies again, hips pumping quick as I find the swell of her clit again, now even more swollen. She lets out a short cry, the noise driving me mad with desire, and it's impossible to keep control anymore when she's making sounds like that.

She comes with a moan of my name that echoes to the ceiling, her nails biting into my chest, and that hot spark of sensation pushes me right over the edge. I lose myself in that orgasm, so much perfect heat milking me to the very last drop as she keeps tightening around me, trying to draw me back in.

"Holy shit, Ava..." I catch my breath in the afterglow, when we're curled up in the center of the bed together. At some point, we manage to disentangle, moving to place our heads on separate pillows, but still watching each other. "I told myself we'd never go this far. Promised myself I wouldn't..."

She laughs, and I can't really blame her. That boundary's well and broken. My cock rests heavily against my belly, still damp with her arousal.

"Guess you should have kept that promise to yourself then."

"Maybe I should have." I bite my tongue, wrestling with the inevitable. "Are you sure it doesn't bother you that I'm leaving tomorrow?"

There's a beat of silence, but she shakes her head. "I'm a sensible girl, I knew this was temporary."

It's not really an answer, and for a moment, the quiet stretches on as I try to figure out what to say. I knew this from the start, that even if anything happened, tomorrow is where it stopped. It's the only thing that makes sense with our lives, with the futures we have planned ahead.

So why does it sting deep inside my chest to hear her verbalize that? Was I expecting her to ask me to stay, or to try something long-distance? A pit settles inside my stomach as the silence stretches on around us.

She gently yawns, and I take that as a sign to head to the bathroom, where I ditch the condom and wash up. When I return to the bedroom, she's already asleep, curled on her side, her face still resting on the pillow, facing where I laid. If she was still awake, I wonder if we'd swap stories about obscure world mysteries or the mating rituals of mammals. It makes me sad to think we won't swap stories like that again.

I pull the duvet comforter over her, and slip in beside her, enjoying this last moment I'll get with her.

The thought of leaving in the morning is a somber one, but it's the only decision I can make.

I'll wake up early and slip out before she's even up. That way there won't be any awkward goodbyes, and we can go on with our lives.

That was always the plan anyway.

Chapter Seventeen

Ava

Lately, it seems like there's a big difference between what I say and what I mean.

I said I wouldn't let things go beyond talking with Barrett, but apparently that meant talking him into bed with me. I couldn't resist a shot at deliciously forbidden sex and half-a-dozen, life-changing orgasms with the man I've lusted after since before I knew what lust was.

I said I wouldn't get attached. I'd kiss him goodbye and then send him back to Chicago, no harm, no foul. Hell, two nights ago, I looked at him, his perfectly sculpted figure lying completely naked in my hotel bed after a night of mind-blowing sex that exceeded any wild dream I had of how good it would be, of how good he would feel…I looked at him and said it didn't bother me that he was leaving. I said things would go right back to normal once he was gone. Apparently what I meant was that I would spend the whole next morning feeling empty, staring at the door, and hoping he'd come right back to me.

It seems so ridiculous, he was only here for a few days. Most of which he spent teasing me right in front of my family. It was practically torture while he was here, but now that he's gone, what I wouldn't give for that smug grin to be tempting every ounce of self-control in me. Every logical bone in my body knows that it's stupid to be hung up on something I knew from the start wasn't built to last, but for once, I want to ignore what's logical and go for what I really want.

"Hello, Ava? Anyone home?"

I blink back into reality to find my mother trying to get my attention from across the table, waving her hands slowly through the air.

"Hi, sorry," I grumble, taking another sip of coffee. "Guess I'm not quite awake yet."

From the way she furrows her brow, it's obvious that Mom isn't buying that. "Are you okay, sweetheart?" she asks, pulling out the chair next to mine and settling in. I'm definitely not in the mood to talk, but that's never stopped her before.

"Yeah, I'm fine. Just worn out from the weekend." Suddenly, I'm deeply interested in my cuticles. Fascinating little things. Or maybe it's just that I don't want Mom to see what's really on my mind.

"Well, as long as you're here, there's something I wanted to talk to you about."

I roll my shoulders back and brace myself. "What's going on, Mom?"

"Well," she sighs, "it's about the factory."

I'm uncertain whether I'm relieved that we're not about to talk about Barrett or exhausted to be having yet another conversation about this.

"There's nothing to talk about with the factory, Mom." I scoot my chair back to get up in a last-ditch effort to dodge this topic, but she lays her hand over mine, squeezing tight.

"Ava, please. Just listen for a minute."

How can I say no to my own mother?

I sit back down.

"First, we're really proud of you for coming and filling your father's shoes. Really. But I've been giving it some thought and the whole thing is really unfair to you.

You shouldn't be living here with us and putting your life on hold just for the sake of a factory that would probably be worth more if you just sold it."

I let out a groan that's been building in the back of my throat since she sat down. "Mom, not you too. You've been talking to Nick, haven't you?"

"Well, he makes some good points," she admits. "He just wants to see you happy. We all do. I mean, giving up your own apartment and your job just for a family business that might not even make it? It's just not fair to you, sweetie. You should be out living a life of your own, starting a family of your own."

"And I will. You know that starting a family isn't on my list right now, Mom."

"That's not how falling in love works, Ava." Mom has shifted into her infamous lecturing voice. "It's not something you put on a list. It happens at the right time when you open yourself up to it. You can't do that if you're living at home and trying to hold together a failing factory. You can't just decide when you're going to cross love off your to-do list."

"Well, right now that's how it has to be." I can hear the anger building in the tightness of my voice. I've never yelled at my mother, and I'm not about to start now. I try again, calmer, quieter. "It can't be a priority right now when there are other things that need to come first."

The kitchen is silent for a moment as Mom rests her head in her hands, gathering herself with a few deep sighs.

"He called and asked for you, you know."

I freeze mid-sip of coffee. She lifts her head just enough that I can see the slightest smile creep across her mouth. It's enough for me to worry she's talking about who I secretly want her to be talking about.

"Who?"

Maybe it's not him. Don't get your hopes up.

"Barrett."

I bite down hard on my bottom lip to steel my nerves. Of course, it's harder to cover up the sound of my heart knocking against the inside of my chest. After a long pause, Mom offers up a bit more context to fill the silence.

"He called yesterday on his drive back, wanted to thank us for letting him stay, and inviting him to the party and all. Then he asked if he could talk to you. I went ahead and gave him your cell phone number."

"Why would you do that?" Apparently, biting my lip only does so much for keeping my mouth shut. Mom chuckles a little under her breath.

"Oh Ava, honey, you don't have to bother with pretending. I'm your mother, for heaven's sake. I see the way you've looked at Barrett since you were in middle school. You had that same look in your eyes all weekend."

"I can't believe you're encouraging this, Mom. You should be mad at me."

"Mad? Why? Barrett's a good man. A great man."

"Sure, a great man who also happens to be Nick's best friend."

"So?" She looks genuinely confused. Does she really not get it?

"So, Nick would be furious. Which is why things have to end here."

I jump to my feet and snatch my coat from the back of the chair, making it clear that this conversation is over.

"I need to get to work," I call out over my shoulder as I pull on my boots and fling open the front door. I don't care that I'm an hour early; I need to get out of this house. You don't run a successful business by sitting at the kitchen table arguing with your mother over the things you can't have.

This time, when I put my key in the ignition, my car whirs to a start without a single stutter. I mentally thank whatever powers of the universe that are in charge of car troubles for showing me a little mercy. God knows I'm not going to catch a break anywhere else today.

When I arrive at the factory, I'm one of only five or six cars in the parking lot. The only employees who come in this early are the maintenance guys who make sure everything is in order for the start of the workday. A few cleansing breaths later, I shift into business mode. This week has been the start of the operation completely under my management, with no help from Dad. I don't have any spare bandwidth to dedicate to Barrett. I'm the boss now, and it's time to act like it.

Other than a few machinery upgrades and a nicer coffee maker in the break room, the factory looks nearly the same as the day Dad first brought me here as a little girl. At the time, the enormous industrial building seemed like an endless steel playground to explore. Now that it's my responsibility, the size of the place makes it a little more daunting and a lot less magical.

There's comfort in the familiar faces, though. Some of the workers have been here so long that they still know me as the six-year-old visiting her dad's office after kindergarten. Being at the factory feels like being around family, only this family doesn't nag me about my romantic life. This family does, however, depend on me to keep this place open and it's time to get my mind back on track.

I'm barely five steps into the building when Mark, a maintenance engineer who has worked here for as long as I can remember, steps out from behind a piece of machinery and gives me a defeated wave. It seems a little early to already be facing a problem, but then again, I seem to be having that kind of day.

"Sorry to hit you with bad news first thing, Ava, but the engine on the belt-line is completely burnt out," Mark mutters, shaking his head and wiping thick black grease onto his jeans. "I've been working on it for a solid hour now, but the thing just isn't moving. We're gonna have to get an order in for a new one today."

"Thanks for working on it, Mark. Just let me know exactly which part to order and I'll get it taken care of." My calm, cool response surprises me a bit. I must have let all my frustration out on Mom. The mechanical side of the factory isn't really in my wheelhouse, but at least this is a problem with a clear-cut solution. Mark leads me over to the conveyor belt and I jot down the name and model of the engine that needs replacing, assuring him I'll have it taken care of before the day is out.

There's something peaceful about being here—this noisy building, the faint scent of oil in the air. I've worked here off and on since I was thirteen and started sweeping floors after school. It's more of a blessing than I ever realized it would be. Rather than resenting their new twenty-five-year old boss, the employees respect me because of all the hours I've put into this place. There was no job too big, or too small for me growing up, I did everything from mopping the floors, to cleaning the toilets, to learning how to turn a wrench.

When I head toward the second floor where the offices are located, it's still a pleasant surprise to see my name on the door of Dad's old office. Sitting in his chair and booting up his computer, I have to keep reminding myself that these aren't his things anymore, but mine. Yes, Dad will be there to answer questions when I run into problems, but the paperwork is signed, the business cards are printed, and this is my factory, my motor that needs replacing, my employees who are relying on me to keep this business running. It's the most gratifying thing in my life right now, and I'm going to make damn sure it succeeds.

I pull up the spreadsheet for the year-end budget and start pricing out replacement engines. With each click on a different retailer's website, the lump in the base of my throat gets bigger and bigger. Who knew engines were this expensive? No matter how I fudge these numbers, the money for a replacement motor just isn't in the budget. How much had Dad been cutting his own salary, or worse yet, paying out of pocket to keep this company going? I open file after file of budgets from every quarter, crunching numbers and looking for where Dad was able to cut back. The numbers are tight. For the first time, an errant thought that maybe Nick was right flits through my brain.

"How are things looking, Ava?"

Mark peeks his head into the office. The smile on his face is hopeful, cautiously confident. I remember how Mark used to let me hold the wrenches when I was little while he did simple repairs on the machinery. He's a bit younger than Dad and, from what I remember, still putting his kids through college. I can't let him down.

"Things are looking great." I fake a smile and press the button to place the order for the engine. I'm going to make this work no matter what I have to do. "We should be in good shape to get this thing installed as soon it arrives. Let's go assess how everything else is running in the meantime." I close out of the spreadsheets and put the computer into sleep mode. One thing at a time.

It's a quarter after seven by the time I finish taking stock of the factory equipment with Mark and the other maintenance workers. I apologize profusely for keeping them so late, but they're grateful when I give them clearance to leave a bit earlier tomorrow after the new engine is up and running. As for me, I'll be awake all night trying to cut costs somewhere in the budget to keep us in the black. The work may be stressful, but at least it's enough to keep me completely distracted. I forgo the radio in the car and instead spend the drive home doing mental math. I already gave up my apartment to save on rent by staying with Mom and Dad. What's next?

The engine runs as I sit parked in the driveway, running options through my head until my buzzing phone interrupts my thought process. It's a text message and when I look down and read it, I have to blink twice, to be sure I'm reading it right.

        Can't stop thinking about the other night.

It's Barrett. My heart trips over itself in an effort to speed up. My smile is immediate, but I can't help but tease him.

That bad, huh?

It takes him a second to reply, but my smile still refuses to fade as I watch the screen.

Best night of my life.

My fingers fly over the keys, tapping out a reply before my brain can filter it.

Mine, too.

I like that we're being honest, that we're not hiding behind the truth of what we did. And the truth is, it was a magical night. By far the best sex of my life, but it was more than that, too. When I was with him it was like nothing else in the world mattered—I didn't think once about the weight of my obligations, about work or my family. I could just be myself, and he liked me just the way I was. It was so easy to make him laugh, or smile, or to please him in bed.

And I'm not going to lie, there's something incredibly sexy about being with an older man, about letting him show me the ropes, the way he looked at me was almost worshipful, like I was pure sin but worth going to hell for every minute he was inside of me.

Well ... next time you're back in Indiana ...

I type the message, and stare at it for a full minute, then hit delete before I accidentally send that message.

It was a one-time thing. A flash of lightning in an otherwise dark night. Let it go, Ava.

But then another message pops up on my screen, and I realize, with my heart in my throat, it could change everything.

Come to Chicago this weekend?

Wouldn't that be like playing with fire, delaying the inevitable heartbreak this fling will surely result in?

When I don't reply three minutes later, he calls me. I let the phone ring twice, then take a deep breath before answering his call.

"Didn't scare you off, did I?" Barrett's rich voice pours through the phone and straight inside me. I can hear him smiling through the phone.

My toes curl in my shoes, and I open my mouth to respond, but my breath wavers and, "Hi, Barrett," is all I can manage.

"I had a great weekend with you," he says, voice low and teasing.

Memories of our stolen kisses, of teasing him and fleeting glances shared across the room. Of his muscular body moving over mine, and the deep, sexy groan that tumbled from his lips when he finally pushed inside. My nipples pebble inside the lace cups of my bra, and my breathing grows ragged at the memory that's still so fresh in my mind that I swear I can feel him.

"I did, too," I admit, voice soft.

"Then you should say yes. Ava…come spend the weekend with me."

Chapter Eighteen

Ava

I'm nervous.

I ease my car into a parking spot and crane my neck to look up.

Even from where I'm parked a few blocks away, the enormous silver tower that I'm almost positive is Barrett's building stands taller than everything else around it.

Part of me still can't believe I'm actually doing this. The three-hour drive passed by quickly with an audiobook about the Nepalese people of Katmandu. But now I'm here, and the anxiety of highway driving in a large city like Chicago subsides to make room for a new kind of nervous, a Barrett kind of nervous.

Suddenly, the trip out seems a lot less scary than telling him that I'm here. I fumble for my phone, reminding myself that *he* is the one who invited *me*. He wants me here. He wants to see me. Just call him already. My fingers tremble, but I manage to press his name on my phone. Not even half a ring later, he picks up.

"Hello?"

I haven't heard his voice since he invited me a couple of days ago, and just one "hello" is all it takes for my cheeks to heat up and my toes to curl. Keep your cool, Ava.

"Hey, I'm here," I say, trying to even my breath behind my shaking voice.

"Great, I'll come get you. Where are you parked?"

I list off a few of the names of the shops I'm parked by.

"Be out in a sec."

Butterflies take flight in my stomach. It still doesn't feel real that I'm about to see him again. And this time there will be no meddling parents—or my brother—in our way. The reality of it doesn't completely hit me until I spot him across the street. I could recognize that sculpted frame from a mile away, his black jacket zipped tight so that the fabric stretches across his broad shoulders. He's wearing a fitted pair of dark wash jeans cuffed just above a pair of dark brown boots, the same color as his hair, which is somehow untouched by the reckless Chicago wind. My heart clenches in my chest. I knew I missed him, I just didn't realize how much.

When I step out of the car, Barrett shoots me a smile that lights up his entire face and makes my knees weak.

"You made it," he says, pulling me in for a quick hug, which is all we can safely manage before the oncoming traffic starts laying on the horn. "Come on, let's get out of the cold." He takes one of my gloved hands in his and leads me down the block to his building, which seems even bigger up close.

"After you," he says, gesturing toward the revolving doors, which officially make this apartment building fancier than a lot of hotels I've stayed in. The foyer of the building reflects that sentiment with its leather couches and marble floors.

I had assumed his place would be nice, but nothing I dreamt up during my three-hour drive quite lived up to this. An apartment with a front desk attendant? I didn't even know that existed. Between this fancy apartment and his plush job at the law firm, why would he ever leave Chicago? A lump forms in my throat at the thought, but I force it down. No time to deal with the distance thing right now.

"Have you been doing alright?" he asks, leading me into an elevator. "When I talked to your mom, she couldn't stop talking about how worried she is about you. Said you're working yourself to the bone at the factory."

I roll my eyes. Of course, Mom talked to him about the factory.

"She sounded so worked up about it. I figured I'd better get you out of the house and away from work for a bit. Maybe it'll do both you and your mom some good."

"So, you invited me here because of my mother? That's hot."

He laughs.

I try not to sound too defeated, but I could hear the disappointment in my voice. Why had I bothered wearing my sexiest underthings if this was nothing more than a favor for my mom?

The elevator dings and the doors part to reveal a navy blue carpeted hallway gently lit with a warm yellow glow. I follow Barrett to the third apartment door on the left, which he swiftly unlocks.

"Come inside," he says as I cross through the door, but I hardly have the time to give the place a once over before he closes the door and takes my jaw in his large hands, pulling me into a fiery hot kiss. Maybe my sexy panties weren't such a bad idea after all.

I part my lips to welcome his tongue, which strokes and twirls around mine. The fact that I went even a week without this is unbelievable. Barrett weaves one hand through my hair while the other latches onto the wool coat I dug out of the garage, keeping me locked tight against his chest. He softly tugs my lower lip with his teeth, releasing me just enough that I can catch half a breath.

"Does that feel like your mother has anything to do with this?"

My smirk matches his. "I guess not," I whisper.

"You guess?" he says, one eyebrow cocked. "Well then, let's take the guesswork out of it."

Barrett presses me against the door, kissing me again and again, each kiss more demanding than the last. Our hands work in a frenzy, shedding layers, leaving behind a trail of boots, coats, gloves, scarves, all tumbling onto his apartment floor. He takes a step back to admire me, dressed casually in a pair of skinny jeans and a fitted, long-sleeved t-shirt. His large hands span my waist, his thumbs pressed to my hips. My body is already tingling.

"I don't want to rush this. We need a time out. Come here." Taking my hand, he tugs me into the living room where we sit down on the couch.

His place is nice, it's small but cozy with a gray couch and matching ottoman, a rustic wood dining table piled with work papers and his laptop. There are framed photos lining the bookshelf across the room, mostly shots of him and Nick, or other groups of guys doing various outdoor sports. None of a woman, other than his mother, which I think is a good thing.

"A time out?" I ask, raising one brow.

"I just think we should talk. We jumped into this, and…. *What?*" He's smiling.

I realize my brows are scrunched together, and I'm giving him a confused look. "I'm sorry. I'm not used to guys who want to *talk*. Please continue."

He takes my hand, and laces our fingers together. "I'm not a guy, Ava. I'm a man. A man who is very, very interested in taking you to bed, but I happen to think consent is sexy as fuck."

I swallow and wait for him to continue while my belly tenses with butterflies yet again.

"So, you're going to be the one calling the shots here," he says meeting my eyes with a serious expression. "I know how much I'm risking by having you here, and I've come to terms with that. But you're risking something, too, and I need to know you're okay with that."

He's afraid he's going to hurt me, that this is all going to end in disaster.

I'm struck by a flurry of emotions all at once. Suddenly I know that once this forbidden fling ends, I won't bounce back like I usually do after a breakup—by eating double-stuffed cookies and writing in my journal. No, this is something altogether different.

I haven't wanted to admit it, but something much bigger than I ever expected is happening between us, but before I can ponder it further, Barrett leans in and presses a soft kiss to my lips.

"Say something, Ava. I'm a big boy, whatever it is, I can handle it."

I draw a deep breath, fighting to unscramble my thoughts and focus on the man in front of me. The man who wants me. "If you think for one second I'm walking away from this…"

I don't even finish the sentence before his lips crash down on mine.

He kisses me like I've never been kissed before, sucking on my tongue, nipping at my lower lip. I push my fingers into the hair at the back of his neck, my tongue twisting with his.

"Tell me," he manages.

Another kiss interrupts him.

"What you…"

His mouth hovers over mine.

"Want."

Barrett pulls back, looking at me.

There is so much fire in that crystal clear blue gaze that it momentarily renders me speechless.

"You." Is all I manage before he hoists me up from the couch. We only make it so far as the hallway before he sets me down and pins me against the wall. I'm just as crazed with want. I push my hands under his shirt, touching his chest, his abs, any patch of bare skin I can get my hands on.

He wastes no time peeling off my shirt until I'm standing before him in a lacy bra and just my jeans.

"Jesus, Ava."

My heart is hammering out of my chest, and the hungry look in his eyes makes me feel oddly emotional. "What?"

"You're so damn sexy."

I've never been described as sexy in my entire life, but he makes me feel like I am. Then he's unbuttoning my jeans, and I can feel myself tighten a bit as he grazes the precious space between my thighs. Once he's stripped me down to his liking, he grips my ass with sturdy hands, his touch becoming reacquainted with my curves.

If he notices that I deliberately took the time to match my bra to my panties, he certainly doesn't stop to comment. His mouth is a little occupied working its way down my neck, decorating my skin with little pink circles on his journey down to my breasts. Good God, are we going to do this right here in the hallway? With this whole apartment at our disposal?

Before I can contemplate that further, he lifts me up by my ass and hoists me up onto him. I can't help but giggle the tiniest bit as I lace my legs around his waist. I hold tight to his shirt, using it as an excuse to feel his sculpted pecs through the thin material as he carries me to the kitchen, his mouth still devouring mine.

He lowers me onto the granite countertop, then pulls back to meet my eyes. Using the pads of his fingers, he strokes my cheek so gently, so softly as he gazes down at me.

"You are so beautiful. I'm glad you came."

Of course, I came but it'd be too much to admit that I missed him. Too intimate. So instead I pull him in for another kiss.

His hands slip down to my waist, and he holds me close as our tongues twirl and glide together.

When I'm breathless, he pulls back again, meeting my eyes. "I'm sorry I just left the hotel. You were asleep, and…it just seemed like the best way."

I nod. "A clean break. I get it. Except…"

His mouth quirks up in a lopsided grin. "I needed another taste."

Our lips crash together again, but I sense the time for talking is done, because this time, his fingers trace circles over my skin, caressing and stroking me from my shoulders to my arms to my lower back. And then his lips are on my neck, his teeth grazing my collarbone, moving lower until his hands are cupping my breasts and his mouth is leaving damp kisses along my cleavage.

When I reach back to unclasp my bra, he pauses, waiting in anticipation as I peel the lace away from my skin and let it drop to the tile floor.

His gaze is almost worshipful as he takes in the sight of my bare breasts—barely a B cup, but so high and perky I really don't even need a bra.

"Shit," he curses under his breath. "These are fucking amazing." His thumb grazes the tip of one breast and I barely hold in a shudder.

Every time we're together it's as if he has all the time in the world to tease and toy with my body. The slow touches, the drawn-out foreplay, the laser focus on my orgasm. Meanwhile, I feel like I'll die if I don't feel him inside me in the next four seconds.

I reach in between us and palm the erection I can feel through his jeans.

"Oh fuck, please," I whimper as he hooks his fingers inside my panties, stroking me lightly with the backs of his knuckles.

"Please what?" he breathes into my ear. His voice is hot, sinful, and dripping with pure sex.

I meet his gaze, blinking at him, innocently. "Please fuck me with that big cock of yours, Barrett."

He releases a groan of approval. I guess he likes my dirty talk.

And it's all the invitation he needs. A quick tug on his boxer briefs and his erection springs free. Glad to see he's just as excited to see me as I am to see him. His briefs fall to the floor and he begins rubbing the head of his erection against my opening. Yes, yes, yes. My toes curl at how very right this feels. God, I don't think I'll ever get over how big he is.

"Fuck." He pulls away.

"What's wrong?" I look up at him, suddenly confused.

"I need to go grab a condom. Don't move."

I wrap my hands around his waist, not letting him move. "Do we need one?" I'm on birth control, and there's no one I trust more than Barrett.

His eyes meet mine. "Never done that before."

"Ever?" I blink at him.

He shakes his head, and I can see that he's telling me the truth. Which is crazy, he's thirty years old.

"Well, I'm on the pill, and I've only been with two men, and I've been tested, and I haven't slept with anyone in over a year." *Oh my God, why am I babbling?* I place my hand on his cheek and meet his eyes. "I'm good if you are."

For a moment, I'm not sure what he's thinking, and then he presses a tender kiss to my lips. "Just that you'd trust me with this is…" He gives me another kiss. "Yes."

Taking a firm hold of my hips, he pulls me to the edge of the counter and parts my thighs as wide as they will go. I'm perfectly positioned to take all of him, and I have a feeling that's exactly what he's going to give me.

One smooth, very slow thrust, and my eyes dart up to his. The look of focus on his face is almost breathtaking. He's biting into his lower lip, his eyes half-lidded in concentration.

Barret slides in farther, and I yelp a little.

He pulls back immediately, a concerned look flashing across his handsome features. "Fuck." He cups my cheek with his large palm, his regret instant. "I'm so, so sorry. Are you okay?"

"It's okay." I nod. "Just maybe go a little slower."

His eyebrows are still scrunched together when he leans down and presses a tender kiss to my mouth. "I can't seem to control myself around you. I'll be careful, okay?"

I nod again, smiling at him so he knows it really is okay.

He starts again, setting a slower pace, and dear God, this man must have the patience of a saint because after several minutes of this slow-tempo lovemaking, I'm ready to burst.

He's so much to take, but it feels like heaven. I rock my hips to match his thrusts, letting him push deeper and deeper into me.

"You ready for more?" he asks, his eyes falling down to where our bodies are joined. My gaze follows and holy hell, the sight is so erotic. His manhood is painted in my arousal, and I can see he hasn't been giving me his whole length, just pushing into me until my toes curl, and then retreating.

Again, the patience of a saint.

"More," I confirm on a groan, lacing my fingers behind his back and pulling him in deeper.

He obeys, his rhythm kicking up, and soon he's thrusting into me as far as he can go and I moan so loud I'm running the risk of neighbors calling in a noise complaint. Let them call, I don't give a damn. This feels too good to stop.

I tuck my pelvis just right so that he slides up against my g-spot and all of me tightens and contracts. Shit, I thought the sex was amazing our first time; but this is on another level. Maybe it's just that every time with him gets better. With each of his thrusts, my body tenses and my breath escapes me, my heart thumping in double time.

"B-Barrett! God, yes, Barrett!" I pant as he pushes so deep into me that I finally unravel. With one last stutter of his name, I come while he is still pressed deep into me. He grunts as I contract and release around him, still rocking in and out of my pulsing heat.

Instead of giving me a second to catch my breath, he scoops my still-trembling frame off the counter and sets me on my feet, bent over the kitchen sink this time.

His lips are at the back of my neck. "Can you stand?"

I nod, and tentatively he moves his hands from my hips, making sure he can trust me. I grip the counter in front of me, and feel his erection brush against my ass.

Steadying himself with one hand locked to my shoulder, he presses into me from behind, hitting totally different parts of me. He groans and I contract around him again at the sound of him losing control. I push back a bit, rocking back onto his stiff length, which he gives another approving groan to.

I can feel his muscles tightening as he teeters on the edge of climax. With an arch of my back, he slides so deep into me that I can practically feel him behind my belly button. Using my body as though I weigh nothing at all, he pulls me back onto him again and again.

"Where should I come?" he asks.

"Inside me."

I can hear his breath choke and he empties into me with a final trembling thrust. Once he eases out of me, I turn around to place a grateful kiss on his mouth. He gathers me up in his arms, pulling me close to his chest.

"Welcome to Chicago," he whispers against my hair.

I smile and run my hand down the scruff on his cheek. If I go even a second without touching him I'm afraid I'll snap out of whatever perfect dream I'm in and he'll disappear. As long as I'm touching him, this has to be real.

He tilts up my chin with the tips of his fingers to press his mouth against mine. Unlike every kiss we have shared up until this moment, this kiss is delicate and sweet. This kiss doesn't say "I want to bend you over on my coffee table," although I know he does—and probably will later this evening. This kiss says, "I'm happy you're here," and when he pulls away, the gentleness of it sends a tingle down my spine.

"I've got you for two full days," he says, playfully tucking my messy sex hair behind my ear. "And I promise to make it to the bedroom next time."

A shudder vibrates through me. Being back with him has been so absolutely perfect already that I almost forgot that I only have him for two short days. Forty-eight hours in an incredible city with the grown-up version of my childhood boy crush, then I'll be back on the road, pushed out of this dream state and back into reality, aka Indiana. And I'll have three hours of driving to replay a weekend's worth of memories before letting them go, leaving them somewhere in the snow on the side of the highway.

As unfair as it seems, I can't bring any of it with me. This isn't just some high school fantasy anymore. This is real life. And at the end of the day, I have to keep telling myself that Barrett's life is here in Chicago, and mine is in a factory in the middle of nowhere. Some lives aren't meant to line up, no matter how much I desperately wish they could.

This is why I was scared to start this in the first place. Why I wanted to cut things off when he went back to the city. Why I fled the car in a panic that night in my parents' driveway—the first time things turned physical between us.

It's because I knew from the very beginning that just a little would never be enough, that the second I got the slightest taste of Barrett, I would start falling in love.

Chapter Nineteen

Barrett

After doing perfectly ordinary things during the day with Ava, like watching a movie, going to the grocery store, and visiting a bookstore, I've scored us a reservation at my favorite tapas restaurant for dinner tonight. But it's not just a great meal that has me looking forward to the evening—it's the chance to spend more time with her.

After ushering her inside, my hand resting on the small of her back, I guide us to the hostess station. A few heads turn in our direction, and I can't help but wonder what people think when they look at us together. Do they think we're a couple? Shit, are we a couple? I'm guessing they wonder what kind of lucky prick I am to get a girl like her.

She looks flawless tonight in a pair of well-fit jeans that hug her curves, and a bright red sweater that dips low in the front. Her hair is loose over her shoulders, and her blue eyes are done up in eyeliner and mascara. Something inside me likes that she made an extra effort to look good for our date.

We're led to a private table for two with a white tablecloth and a small candle burning in the center. I help Ava into her seat, and then we begin to peruse the menus. Ava unfolds hers with wide eyes, skimming over page after page like she's not sure where to start.

"If you let me order, I promise you'll have the best dinner of your life," I say.

She looks up from the wine menu with a raised brow. "That's a pretty big promise to make."

"I can back it up." When I see her blush, I wonder if we're still talking about dinner, or something else. "What do you say?"

After one more glance at the list of entrees, she folds the menu and sets it on the table. "Ball's in your court, Barrett. Impress me."

That I can do. The look on her face when I rattle off a whole banquet of dishes and matching wines is priceless, but our waitress takes it in stride, promising to be back with our drinks in just a moment.

Our wine is delivered, and Ava tries a sip, testing the merlot on her tongue before swallowing.

"Do you approve?"

"It's delicious," she confirms.

I can't help but notice the heat lingering in her expression as she takes another drink.

"I'm curious," I say, leaning forward. "What kinds of fascinating topics are you studying these days?"

She laughs, her blue eyes brightening as she meets my gaze. "Proboscis monkeys."

I make a questioning expression.

"You know the kind with the big pink noses?" she asks.

I remember back to a nature show I watched once. "I think so. The ones that look like they have a dick coming off their face?"

She rolls her eyes, laughing again. "How old are you again?"

"Thirty."

"Right, of course you are. Anyway, I've been reading about them. They're fascinating. The males make a loud, nasally call with that nose of theirs, and the females will travel long distances in search of the male with the loudest call."

"Sort of like you traveling all the way to Chicago …"

She rolls her eyes, but the irony isn't lost on me.

"So, it's a desirable trait?" I ask, taking another sip of my wine as I watch her.

"Oh yes. The alpha males are often the noisiest of the bunch."

"Sounds fascinating."

Ava nods.

God, she's adorable.

Our food is delivered and we waste no time digging in. There are grilled shrimp, stuffed mushrooms, and seared scallops. And the dishes don't stop coming. I love this restaurant.

"Try this," I say, raising a date stuffed with goat cheese to her lips.

She opens and I place the bite on her tongue. Her eyes widen and lock on mine as she chews. "Oh, my God, that's the best thing I've ever eaten."

"Glad you like it."

Our fingers keep brushing as we pass around the plates, and she has the courage to catch my hand and suck a stray drop of sauce off my thumb.

"That's dangerous," I whisper.

"I know," she says with no small amount of pride, daring me to comment further.

For now, I hold back. It's no fun if she can bait me that easy every time, although it makes dinner an entertaining back-and-forth.

She clings to me on the way out of the restaurant, and I shield her against the harsh wind. The moment we step back into my apartment, I turn up the heat to warm her and she lets out a deep breath of relief.

"Sit and warm up." I can't resist rubbing her back, stealing one more touch. It's still surreal that I get to touch her at all. It's not something I'm going to take for granted. "I'll be right back."

Her curious look follows me all the way to the kitchen. Once I'm out of sight, I take a pair of glasses out of the cabinets and fetch the champagne I've kept chilling in the fridge. Stripping away the foil with my thumb on the cork, I let it open slowly, the hiss of pressure fading away by degrees. Once the bubbles have calmed down, I fill both glasses with care, letting the foam rise to the perfect height.

I'm about to carry the champagne in when my phone rings. Setting the glasses back on the counter, I see Nick's number on the screen and pick up. "Hey, man. What's up?"

"Nothing, which is why I'm calling my best friend." When he pauses, I check the time; it's pretty late. "You up for going out? I could use a little action tonight, and I'm guessing you could too."

"Just a second," I say, keeping my voice low so it doesn't carry, and step farther into the kitchen.

On any other night I'd say yes, blowing off steam before another week of the grind at the firm, but not with Ava in the other room. Not with his sister here, who I've been shacking up with since last night. I run my hand over the counter, remembering Ava's arms around me as she hit her peak, gasping for me to stay inside just a little longer.

"Sorry, I've got my hands full here." I put as much innuendo in the words as I dare, hoping he'll get my meaning fast.

He laughs. "*Oh*, I see. You've got some hot piece waiting in the other room with her panties off and I'm keeping you occupied."

I wince, glad he can't see it from his end of the line. If he had any idea whom he was talking about, he'd be embarrassed out of his mind—right before he slugged me in the mouth. "Yeah, something like that. I've got to go."

He sighs, but doesn't push the issue. "Okay, okay. Have fun, man. 'Night."

Shaking my head like it'll wipe away the conversation, I carry the glasses of champagne into the living room. Ava lights up as I sit down next to her, and I'm trying to think of a good toast when she leans over to kiss me.

"Does this mean we're having a quiet night in?" she asks, her lips a breath away from mine.

"We could go out, but that would mean sharing you with everyone else." My eyes lock with hers. "I don't want to do that. I'm going to be selfish and keep you all to myself until tomorrow."

She smiles, fingers brushing against my knee before she settles back in her seat to take a long sip of the champagne. "Mm. Was that my brother you were talking to in there?"

I'd hoped that Ava hadn't heard, but there was no point in lying to her. "Yeah, he wanted to go out."

"He's not going to come over, is he?" Worry trickles into her voice.

"No, I told him I had someone over."

"Oh." She looks relieved, but not really surprised. "I suppose he's used to you having women over."

Not so much in recent days, although it's true enough that I don't try and argue. We share the champagne instead, trading sips until I can't stand to not be touching her anymore. Her glass clinks against the table as I set it down beside mine. Then I gather her close and press a soft kiss to her lips.

"Thank you for coming this weekend, baby," the words roll off my lips before I can stop them, but I mean it. The sentiment is too true to deny.

"Thank you for having me," she whispers back, and suddenly having her is the only thought in my mind.

She follows my lead, rising from the couch, and heat sparks between each kiss as I guide her toward my bedroom.

Once inside, I flip on the small lamp beside my bed.

She gives me a questioning look. "What's that for?"

I bring my hand to her cheek, stroking her skin. "You're incredible, and I want to see all of you."

Her chin dips down as she looks at her toes. For the first time, I truly realize that she may not be all that experienced in the bedroom. She told me about the fact she'd only been with two other men, but I hadn't really considered her past. Despite her false bravado, the confidence she has about asking for what she wants, I like the idea that there haven't been many men before me. Maybe it means I can leave a lasting mark, that no one who comes after me could quite compare. Misogynistic, but there it is.

Lifting her chin with two fingers, I meet her eyes and take her mouth again.

The fact that we just have tonight left to ourselves sticks under my skin like a thorn. Every time I touch her, she gives me more and more, but somehow it isn't enough. I don't know what *enough* would be, but right now it's getting her naked and lying her back against the pillows.

She doesn't let me indulge in the sight for long, pulling me down into another kiss as I find the clasp to her bra and slip it open. Her hands caress down my chest, searching for every bare inch of skin she can find until brushing against the bulge inside my pants.

"Take these off." She tugs at my jeans.

I obey, stripping down completely before joining her on the bed again.

Her eyes immediately drop to my lap, and I have to stifle a chuckle. I'm glad she seems to be just as pleased with my body as I am hers.

As her fingers wrap around the base of me and squeeze, sparks of pleasure ignite through my body.

A moan escapes her lips when my fingers find her wet, drawing circles along her silken flesh until she gasps, "Barrett, I'm ready for you."

My entire body aches at those words, and I know she means it, even if I still have to start slow, sinking into the hot velvet of her warmth in one controlled thrust at a time. Her nails bite into my hips as every inch fills her, and I trail kisses from her throat to the fullness of her lips, waiting for her breathing to steady before I start to move.

Her hips rock into the rhythm with mine, drawing me in as deep as I can go. I slide an arm between her back and the sheets so I can hold us together, not wanting her to escape me for even a second.

"You feel amazing," I murmur against her ear. "How am I ever supposed to stop?"

"I don't want you to stop," she moans, and clenches tight around my shaft as if it will keep me there forever.

Sounds perfect to me.

The faster I move, the louder she gets, and Ava comes while looking me right in the eyes, wonder written all over her face. Her orgasm snaps the last thread of my control, the world going white as ecstasy overtakes everything else and runs wild through my body. I pull her into kiss after breathless kiss, lingering in the afterglow.

We spend a long time like that, with our bodies tangled together, our hands interlaced as we study the size difference between them. After a while, I can see she's sleepy, and I wrap her tightly in my arms, the sheets tugged up just over our hips.

"This almost feels like a dream," she murmurs, so soft that I don't think I was supposed to hear it.

* * *

My ringtone for work jolts me awake, and I scramble to get my phone from where it's tucked in my pants before it goes to voicemail. I've had a rare work free weekend. It's Sunday, but that doesn't mean the partners expect me to sound anything except sober and alert.

"Mr. Lyons, good morning," I say, calling up a professional smile. Even if he can't see, it puts me in the right frame of mind.

"Barrett." Lyons' voice rumbles over the line, raspy with his age. "I hope you're not wasting the day away."

Glancing to where Ava still lays half-asleep, I can't make myself call it a waste. Sure, we slept in late, but it was after a night I won't be forgetting any time soon. "Of course not, sir."

His chuckle says he might not quite believe me, but is too polite to say otherwise. "We need you in the office ASAP. One of the juniors you staffed on Promenades deal just called in sick."

I rack my mind over the work assignments for the deal, forcing my eyes away from Ava for just a minute. "Okay…"

"I need your eyes on the merger agreement now. We're on a strict timeline. I need everything on my desk first thing tomorrow morning." *Strict* meaning the client would walk away if we don't jump to make them happy fast. "I know you're looking for more responsibility, now's the time to prove it."

Shit. That's an offer with an expiration date. "In and out in a in a few hours?"

"As long as you cross your t's and make it look neat and it's on my desk tomorrow morning, I couldn't care less how long it takes you.," Lyons says.

If this was any other Sunday, I wouldn't even have to think about it, but Ava's here. Even if it will kill me to cut our weekend short, I know what I need to do. "I'll be there in an hour, sir."

"Excellent. Knew I could count on you."

The line goes dead and I sigh, tossing my phone back onto the bedside table. Ava stirs at the sound, so effortlessly beautiful even while half awake. I'd planned to spend the morning with her, enjoying every last second until she had to leave, but that's out of the question now.

"What's the frown for?" she asks.

"I've got to head into work. There's a client emergency."

She frowns, too, but she sits up enough to give me a kiss. "That's okay. I have to drive back anyway."

Our weekend went so fast and I'm at a mental crossroads with no clear direction, stuck between wanting to keep Ava in my bed and my duties at work. Climbing the corporate ladder doesn't happen on its own and I know this. So, rather than deal with the emotions of what this is, I go with the physical instead. Looking over at Ava, I smile and say, "Shower with me?"

Chapter Twenty

Ava

Barrett pulls me into his arms under the warm spray of water, and we just stand there, enjoying the feel of our bodies pressed together.

"Temperature okay?" he asks.

I nod, tightening my arms around his waist, and pressing my cheek against his muscled chest.

This weekend has been amazing, and though I'm sad it's almost over, I regret nothing.

As Barrett rubs mint body wash over my skin I close my eyes and savor the moment. He's warm and solid, and so careful with me. It's refreshing how he seems genuinely interested in what I have to say, how he loves my passion for keeping the factory alive. It's like he just gets me.

I could so easily fall in love with this man. The thought slams into me with the force of a freight train, screeching and slamming right into the station. But once the idea has lodged itself in my brain, it's hard to shake. He's a giver in bed. And dear God, his body? He's so sexy it should be illegal. But it's so much more than that, too. He's smart, funny, he has the patience of a saint. Not to mention he spent last weekend using his free time to help my family, and this weekend making sure every moment was perfect for me.

"You are incredible," Barrett murmurs.

Instead I hear words he hasn't said. Words like *I love you.* And *I want to make you mine.*

I can picture us—happy and in love. Both of us working too much, and making the most of our downtime. Him with hair graying at his temples. A cozy home, babies who we adore.

But I know Barrett. I know his goals, they're just as lofty as mine and incredibly important to him. He wants to make partner. Needs it. Needs to prove that he can do it—both to his family, and to himself that he is something, someone worthy of love and praise. I already know he is.

I blink and force the thoughts away. And if there wasn't this distance, or our careers keeping us apart, it'd be his friendship with my brother.

Which is why it can't ever happen. Barrett and I have no future—I can't mistake this weekend for more than what it is. A few orgasms shared between a couple of cool people is not a foundation for a future. Putting on a brave face, I say the only thing I can think of.

"Pass the shampoo?" I say, blinking back the tears that threaten before he can see them.

Chapter Twenty-one

Ava

My weekend in Chicago was nothing short of magical, which has only made this week at work a million times harder.

I sigh heavily, and stare blankly at my computer screen.

I've somehow made it to Friday, but the amount of work I've actually done this week is up for debate. Every hour or so, I get up from my desk and wander through the warehouse, as if the physical movement will stop the intimate images that are on replay through my brain.

Once I'm back at my desk, I can only focus on budgets and spreadsheets for so long before my mind starts to wander. Luckily, this weekend gave me a whole lot of daydreaming material. Between the sex and just enjoying his company, the entire visit had been a dream come true from start to finish. But out of all the incredible memories we crammed into one weekend, my mind keeps returning to my last night there.

Sex with Barrett was always fueled by an unbridled intensity, but the way we made love our last night together was something above and beyond. The way we clung to each other felt desperate, like we knew what we had could slip away at any second.

As I relive it in my memory for the hundredth time, the tears I've been waiting on all week well up in my eyes. That night, Barrett made love to me like he knew we had an expiration date just around the corner. And now, with that expiration date in the rearview, I'm stuck at my desk, dreaming about some universe where every kiss with Barrett isn't on borrowed time.

"Knock, knock!"

The mess of fiery red curls in the doorframe pulls me out of my head.

"Megan, what are you doing here?" I wipe a stray tear from my cheek and try to blink away the heartbroken look in my eyes, but her brows are already scrunched together in suspicion. There's just no fooling your best friend.

"I thought I'd swing by on my lunch break to hear about your weekend with Barrett." Even hearing his name said out loud is enough for my eyes to well up again, which she takes as a signal to shut my door. "Why the tears? Did things not go well? Do you need me to call his office line and chew him out?"

I crack a half smile, wiping a tear from my cheek with the back of my hand.

"No, no. Everything was fine. More than fine, actually. Perfect. That's the problem. He was sweet and romantic and passionate. And now it's over and he's hundreds of miles away."

She pulls a chair around to my side of the desk so we can sit knee to knee.

"I just don't see any way this ends well," I manage to say through sniffles. She grabs the whole box of tissues off my desk and I cradle it in my lap, pulling out tissue after tissue to try to dab up my tears before they get a chance to smear mascara down my cheeks.

"I don't think I've ever seen you like this. You've got it bad," she says, tossing my accumulated pile of wet tissues into the trashcan.

"I know. And it's so stupid. I knew from the beginning that this was all a terrible idea. Between the distance and how upset it would make Nick, I knew I was asking for trouble. But I did it anyway. I'm falling in love with him. I can't believe how stupid I am."

"Hey. Don't say that about my best friend, okay? You're not stupid. You're human."

"Same thing," I groan, which gets a bubbling laugh out of her.

"Hey. You're gonna be okay," she reassures me. I let out a long, staggered sigh. Deep down, I'm not sure if believe her.

"I've got to get back to my office," she says, getting on her feet. "But call me if you need anything, okay? You know I'm just a few blocks away. I can be here in a flash."

"You're a lifesaver. Thank you again."

As she helps me up to hug me goodbye, the usual grumble of voices and hum of machines suddenly grows louder and more frenzied.

"Press pause on the hugs goodbye," I say, holding up one finger. "I need to check on this."

I do one final check for mascara smears in the mirror inside my desk drawer, and roll my shoulders back. Boss mode. Megan follows close behind me as I stride out of my office with newfound confidence. My love life may be a mess, but I've got a factory to keep in ship shape order. Before I can make it into the assembly area, a worker stops me, his eyes practically popping out of his head.

"Ms. Saunders, I don't know if you want to go in there. It's not for anyone with a weak stomach."

What is he talking about? I push past him, Megan in tow. This is my factory, after all. If there's a problem, I need to know about it.

A small crowd of workers has circled around one spot on the assembly floor, murmuring worriedly, but the crowd parts as they see me approaching. At the center of the throng is Mark, the engine maintenance guy, crouched down on the floor with his arm bent back in a way that no arm should be bent.

"He was trying to unjam the engine," one employee from the crowd explains. My stomach drops. That's the engine I ordered. "The engine fell right on him. His arm was crushed really bad, Ms. Saunders. We've gotta get him to the hospital."

"Megan, call 911," I bark over my shoulder as I crouch down at Mark's side. "We need an ambulance here stat." Megan fumbles for her phone and punches in the numbers, rushing out of the building.

"Everybody shut the machines down and go clean up. We're done here for today."

The staff scatters in their assigned directions, powering down the equipment until the production floor is pin drop silent besides Mark's low, strained groans of pain. I repeat back to him the very same words Megan offered me only moments ago. "Hey. You're going to be okay." I pray to God *he* believes me, because honestly, I'm not sure that I do.

* * *

My stomach is tingling with nerves as I walk through the hospital corridor. "I'm here to see Mark Hayes."

The woman at the front desk pushes her wire-framed glasses up the bridge of her wrinkled nose. "Are you family?"

"No, I'm his boss."

She shifts her gaze down to the binder of paperwork she's half-heartedly flipping through. Could this woman lend me even an ounce of her attention? "Visitation is for family only," she says like she's repeated this exact phrase fourteen billion times.

"He was injured on his job site. And my employees *are* family." I stand my ground, placing the big yellow vase of daisies in my hands on the counter to make it clear that I'm not budging. Her stubborn gaze meets mine, but she backs down first, rolling her eyes and slumping her shoulders.

"Room 1284. Head on back."

I offer up a thankful smile, but she only gives me a twitch of her upper lip. Shouldn't I be the one in a bad mood? I pick up the vase and scuttle down the hall before any other hospital personnel stops me. The curtain on Mark's room is pulled back and he's sitting up in the inclined hospital bed, sporting an enormous white cast on his arm. It's only been a few hours since the accident and the room is already filled with mylar balloons that have

"Get Well Soon!" printed on them and a couple of bouquets.

"Those are nice," Mark says, nodding toward the daisies. I set them on his bedside table, arranging them next to a card signed by the guys at the plant. The corner of my mouth curls into a smile. Those guys move fast.

"It's the least I can do. I really can't apologize enough, Mark."

"I appreciate that, Ava. And the flowers, too."

His appreciation does nothing for the pit of guilt in my stomach, though. I was half hoping that he'd tell me that this wasn't at all my fault, but I know that it is without him pointing fingers. I am the one who ordered that engine, and I was the one who didn't have anyone check to make sure it was installed properly. I'm responsible.

"At least you seem to be in good spirits," I offer. Kind of a lame attempt at a silver lining.

Mark glances at his arm and gives his fingers the tiniest wiggle, proving the whole limb isn't out of commission. "The doctors didn't seem too worried about things, which certainly helps," he says. "They said there are a few smaller fractures, but the break itself is pretty clean."

"Well, I don't want you to worry about anything. Your job, your paycheck, your family. It's all going to be taken care of. Just focus on healing, okay?" As I say it, I realize I haven't the slightest clue how I'm going to make it happen. Can I afford to pay an employee that isn't working? Maybe not, but I'll do the right thing. A little voice in the back of my head points out the other side of this. That I can't afford to be sued.

"Thanks, Ava. And thanks for stopping by."

After Mark and I say our goodbyes, I step out of his hospital room and take my first deep breath of the day. Mark is going to be fine and so am I. He's as good as family, and as long as I treat him that way, I'm not at risk of him taking legal action against the company. Accidents happen, right?

As I round the revolving door, the sterile warmth of the hospital gives way to the cold slap of an Indiana winter night. I start crunching numbers—what's two months' pay for Mark? Will I have to hire a contractor in the meantime? I don't know how much further I can stretch a budget that's already spread paper-thin. How did Dad make this work? He never seemed stressed about money or the factory until the day he got sick and couldn't run it anymore. Or did I just not notice? Did Nick see a side of Dad while we were growing up that I was too young to make sense of?

Hopping into my car, I crank the radio dial all the way up. I don't even care what song is playing. All the noise in my head needs to be drowned out, even if just for the drive home. I allow my mind to wander back to Chicago, back to passionate nights with Barrett where everything was simpler and, for just a few days, I didn't have the weight of a whole company on my shoulders.

* * *

"How about we go see a movie?"

I'm usually in my office at this time on Monday mornings, but I told the guys at the plant to take a three-day weekend after Friday's mess. I need the time to budget and get in touch with a few contractors to help me re-order the engine and get it installed safely. Mom, in her typical crusade against me running the plant, has spent all morning suggesting other ideas about what I should do with my "day off." She insists that I need to relax after all of last week's stress.

I try to remind her that this isn't, by any means, a day off, that I have tons of very important work to do, but it all goes in one ear and out the other. I'm hunched over the desk in the spare bedroom we long ago labeled as Dad's office, running numbers for Mark's next two months of pay. Mom hovers over my shoulder, shaking her head. "I think you need to take a break from this, sweetie. We could go get coffee. I'd pay for us both to get pedicures if you want."

"Mom. I can't take a break right now. Can you please just let me work?"

"All you ever do is work," she grumbles, rolling her eyes. "Maybe you need to go back to Chicago and see Barrett. You were relaxed after that. You need to go out there again."

"What I *need* to do right now Mom, is sort out Mark's workers' comp and hire a contractor. Please, just let me get this done."

The doorbell rings and Mom abandons her post over my shoulder to answer it, backing out of the office with her hands up in surrender. "Fine, fine, do what you need to do. Just don't work yourself to death."

I tune out whatever is happening downstairs and laser in on the insurance document I have pulled up, but not even a minute passes before Mom's voice echoes back up the stairs.

"Ava, honey! It's for you."

I push back from the desk in a huff. Hopefully it's Megan making another surprise visit because I don't think I can muster up the energy to politely turn anyone else away. As I descend the stairs, the stern looking gentleman standing on our front porch is completely unfamiliar to me. Maybe he has the wrong address?

"Ms. Ava Saunders?"

I guess that's a no to the wrong address. He rifles through his briefcase and offers up a packet of paperwork. "You've been served."

What? I snatch the paperwork out of his hands and tear open the seal. The word "summons" stares back at me in thick, daunting letters. I can feel my heartbeat behind my eardrums. Mark is suing me? This has to be some kind of joke. After all this company has given him for the past thirty years?

"You've got to be kidding."

The courier shakes his head and latches his briefcase. "You have thirty days to answer the complaint that is listed for you on the paperwork." With a cordial nod goodbye, he's heading down the driveway, leaving me slack jawed and trembling.

Mom swings the door shut and I can feel her sympathetic stare, but I can't manage to lift my eyes from the paperwork in my shaking hands. We stand like this for a good while before I finally say the only thing that comes to mind.

"What the hell am I supposed to do?"

"Call Barrett," Mom says, as though it were obvious. "He'll know exactly what to do."

Every muscle in my body tightens. She's right, as an attorney, Barrett would easily be able to walk me through this, but we haven't so much as texted since I came back.

How pathetic would it be to come crawling to him looking for free legal advice, admitting that while he's flourishing in the city, my life here in Indiana is falling apart?

"No," I mutter, swallowing the lump in my throat and trying to gulp down any bit of confidence with it. "I can handle this on my own. I don't need Barrett."

I repeat it over and over in my head. *I don't need Barrett, I don't need Barrett, I don't need Barrett.* How many times do I have to repeat that before I actually believe it?

Chapter Twenty-two

Barrett

I told myself after the weekend with Ava that everything with her would stop, but it seems like life has other plans. I find myself standing on her parents' doorstep yet again. After knocking twice, I glance through the window, wondering if she's even home.

Mrs. Saunders is the one who answers, and she's all smiles. "Barrett, I'm so glad you could come! How did you drive down here so fast?"

I was already halfway here, but there's not a chance that I'm going to explain to Ava's mom why that is. "Let's just say I was in the neighborhood. And it seemed like you really needed my expertise."

"You're such a sweet boy," she says, shepherding me inside the house, "or a good man, I should say. It's been a long time since you were a teenager tossing a football in my yard." She chuckles as I follow her inside.

The house smells like she's been baking something, but Ava isn't anywhere in sight. As if reading my mind, she smiles and points up the stairs. "She's in her father's office. Going through old contracts to see if she can make the best of everything."

"Injury claims can be a really tough fight to win, especially if the accident happens on site." I'm not trying to burst her bubble, but there's only so much I can bend the truth in a situation like this. "I'll go talk to her."

I haven't made it two steps before Mrs. Saunders puts a hand on my elbow, worry written all over her face. "You know how stubborn she is. She was just trying to do the right thing by keeping the factory open. Her heart's hanging on her sleeve."

"Yeah." Ava's always tried to be the better person, even when it cost her. Guilt threatens to climb my throat, but I force it back down. This has to be about work, about doing the best at my job, not how I feel about her.

I can't let whatever we have—had, I remind myself— jeopardize everything else. But how am I supposed to play this hand with the cards I've been dealt? There's only two ways this can go, and I'm going to have to make the best of it.

Mrs. Saunders lets me go, and I head up the stairs. The door to the office is open an inch, and it doesn't make a sound as I walk on through. Ava is hunched over the desk with an absolute mountain of papers, but she's so focused, she hasn't noticed me. I knock on the doorframe to get her attention, only to get a sigh in response.

"Mom, how do you expect me to finish all this work when you keep interrupting every five minutes to ask-" Ava spins around in her chair to make her point, dropping the file in her hands the moment she sees me. "Barrett."

"Hi." I smile, the same way I feel compelled to do whenever our eyes meet. Even with exhaustion and stress lining her face, she's so damn beautiful. So young and innocent.

If we were alone, if I was here for a different reason, I'd close the door behind me and pull her into my arms for a lingering kiss.

Ava doesn't return my smile, though. Instead, she bends down and starts picking up the file she dropped, shoulders tensed. "I told my mom not to call you."

"When's the last time your mother listened to you?" I ask.

"Just shy of never," she admits, setting the file back onto the desk.

"I'm not here to be your attorney." That much is the truth, even though the raised eyebrow leveled my way says she doesn't believe me. "How about you just tell me what the problem is?"

"Come on. My mom has to have told you that much." She bites her lip, but I can tell she wants to say everything that's on her mind. "One of the workers at the factory was hurt. It looks like the damage will be permanent."

"Hurt how?" There's a lot of ways a case like this can swing.

"An engine on one of the machines crushed his arm. He said it wasn't that bad, but I guess he was wrong. If that wasn't awful enough, it looks like the safety certificate on the machine expired a month ago. My father's been out sick, but it was still his responsibility, and—now it's mine." She frowns, her shoulders looking so tense that it's taking everything in me not to step over and give her a massage. "He's suing, but if I pay everything he's asking for, the plant goes under. If I don't, there's a possibility he may not be able to work for the rest of his life and his family won't have anything to live on."

"Doesn't sound like there's much room for negotiation," I say. "You have any other options?"

"Burning money in court going back and forth over a case I'll probably lose anyway." She reaches up to try and rub the tension from her brow. "I want to give him the money, Barrett. I don't want his life destroyed because we weren't paying attention. But that means everyone else gets screwed over by the plant falling apart."

Damned if you do, damned if you don't. "I'm not sure what to tell you, Ava."

"That's okay." Her laugh is dry with fatigue. "It's my problem, not yours."

"I hate seeing you like this." I close the distance between us in a few steps, and she rises up out of her seat to meet me. "Come here."

Pulling her into my arms, I exhale when her face comes to rest against my chest. She presses even closer, reaching around my back to return the hug. For a moment she's quiet, taking in deep breaths as a shudder goes through her from head to toe.

"You're so confusing, you know that?" Ava sniffles, but stays exactly where she is. "You keep saying we can't do this, but then you keep doing sweet things, like inviting me to stay with you for the weekend and running down here to try and problem solve with me. What is this?"

I don't have a good answer for that. If I was honest, everything would unravel. "Listen, work has me in an awkward place right now. I thought I was a couple of years out from partner, but they told me I was on the fast track if I can get the deal I'm working on to go through."

She leans back to look at me, shock and happiness lighting up her eyes. "Barrett! That's great. Why do you feel weird about it?"

"Wouldn't you feel a little strange if something you'd been chasing for years just suddenly dropped into your lap with a nice red bow on top?" I ask.

She shrugs. "Yeah, I guess, but I'd still go for it."

With her so close, I can't help myself. I move down to kiss her, wanting to wipe all that worry off her face. She leans up into me, returning the kiss with so much sweetness that I have to savor it, lingering against her lips until she's given me everything.

"I wish things could be different between us," I admit in a whisper.

She opens her mouth to answer when I hear someone coming up the stairs. We immediately step back from each other, and she quickly smooths down her hair before Mrs. Saunders pokes her head into the office.

"Barrett, would you like to stay for dinner?" Mrs. Saunders makes it sound more like a plea than an invitation, but I'm not sure I've ever turned down an opportunity to enjoy her cooking. "The rolls just came out of the oven, and I have enough pot roast for everybody."

"Mom, you invited him," Ava says with a slightly exasperated smile, "you knew exactly how much to make."

Her mother dismisses the accusation with a huff, and I quickly step in to intervene. "Of course. I'd love to stay."

* * *

Mrs. Saunders sets the table as Ava and I sit down next to each other, mashed potatoes and green beans filling the space between the pot roast and rolls. A dish of gravy takes up the other side, and I'm about to reach for my plate when Mr. Saunders comes up from the den.

"I was wondering who I heard walking around up here," he says, then starts hunting through a cabinet until finding an unopened bottle of wine. "It's good to see you, son."

"It's good to see you, too, sir." I watch as Mrs. Saunders passes her husband the corkscrew, but his hands struggle with it some, the tension not quite enough to make it pop open. "Let me get that for you."

He surrenders the bottle with a sigh, shaking his head before sitting down at the table. "I swear, half my body is giving up these days. I guess it's no surprise the factory is doing the same damn thing."

Ava's jaw tenses, and everyone but her father sees it. Her mother hurries to get a few glasses so I can pour the wine, and when I hand the first one to Ava, she thanks me under her breath.

"Let's not think about all of that tonight," I declare, holding up my own glass once all of them are passed around. "How about we have a toast?"

Ava raises her glass, and looks at me. "To?"

I meet her eyes, then look away. "To doing the right thing, no matter where it takes you."

Everyone takes a sip from their glasses, and then plates are filled and we begin to eat. Ava's gaze lingers on mine, as if she's trying to decipher my toast. If only I knew what doing the right thing was.

Even Mr. Saunders relaxes after the wine makes one more round around the table, asking me about my work in Chicago. He's never studied law himself, but whenever I talk about it, I always get the sense that he's really listening. Mrs. Saunders chimes in once in a while, although she mostly looks happy that we're carving through the food.

Once the dishes are taken care of, I thank everyone for dinner, and excuse myself to the door. It's a three-hour drive back home, and there's no way I can let myself stay here tonight, not with Ava so close. She knows it, too, following me to the entryway with a wistful sort of smile on her face.

"Driving back tonight?" she asks.

"I have to. Work in the morning." I was barely able to pull enough coverage tonight, and I've made my promises. Breaking them just isn't in the cards.

She steals a look over her shoulder. Both her parents seem occupied in the kitchen, and she takes the opportunity to cup my face and pull me down for a kiss. It's a goodbye without words, the warmth of her mouth and her faint vanilla scent making my chest ache.

"Guess I'll see you later." She runs the back of her knuckles down my shirt, brushing over my abs. "Things always work out like they're supposed to, right? Even if it's not how we planned."

"Exactly." I have to believe that. I have to take the next step forward.

There's a sadness in her eyes when she closes the door behind me, and I'm left standing on the snowy porch by myself feeling empty and alone. Shaking my head, I pull out my keys and start making my way back to the car.

No matter what I might feel inside, this is the way things have to be. She deserves more than I can give her.

Chapter Twenty-three

Ava

To say that things are falling apart isn't exactly true. In order for things to fall apart, things first have to be together, and the more I think about it, I don't think I ever really had things together.

The thought is a depressing one.

I took on this business with blind optimism and a business degree, ignoring all the red flags in favor of looking out for my employees. And where did it get me? In the throes of a legal dispute with next to no money to guide me out.

Sitting at my desk at the factory feels like sitting at mission control for a space launch and slowly realizing there is no fuel in the rocket. I'm not sure if there's any possible way I can get us back to Earth without crashing.

My stomach twists with nerves and I take a deep breath. What I need is a massage.

I read through the court summons for what feels like the thousandth time. It all feels more like an episode of some legal show than my actual life. With the new (correct) engine installed and quadruple checked by the contractor I hired on, the usual sounds of the warehouse have resumed—the low buzz of chatter coupled with the whir of the machinery.

Everything is back to nearly normal for my staff, minus Mark. Word can get around quick in the factory, though. I wonder if any of them know that Mark is suing, if they have any idea what kind of hot water the company is in.

There's a knock on my office door and two imposing men in black suits waltz in, briefcases gripped tightly in their fists. It's awfully rude of them to walk right into my office without letting me answer the door, but the taller of the two men extends one hand across my desk before I have a chance to question their manners. Hesitantly, I stand up and reach my right hand out to meet his.

"Ava Saunders, I presume?" His hand completely swallows mine, more of a power play than a handshake.

"Yes...and you are?"

"Mr. Chase Roland, CEO of Roland Enterprises. This is my colleague. Perhaps you're familiar with our work, we have a factory nearby." Each of them settles into a chair across from my desk, despite the fact that I haven't offered either of them a seat. I hurry back to my desk to shuffle together all the legal papers I had spread out, sliding them into a drawer for later attention. Whoever these men are, my current legal situation is none of their business.

"I can't say I've ever heard of you," I say curtly, which is an obvious blow to Mr. Roland. He wrinkles his forehead, then quickly straightens out his shoulders, regaining his bearings on the conversation.

"Regardless, I'm here today because I'd like to approach you with an offer for this factory of yours."

"Excuse me?" I shift back in my seat, sitting up a bit straighter. "Last I checked it wasn't for sale, Mr. Roland."

"Ava, if I-"

"Ms. Saunders," I correct him sternly.

"Ms. Saunders. I am prepared to offer you a large sum of money for this facility. You have some prime real estate here and I believe my company could turn this into something really valuable. I'm sure we can work out a deal that would be of great benefit to both of us."

"I'm sorry, Mr. Roland, but this plant is invaluable to me. I'm not looking to sell."

"Perhaps you wouldn't feel that way if you were offered a million for this little facility."

I shift my gaze to my feet to try to conceal the surprise in my eyes. A million dollars? That's double the offer I could have imagined in my wildest dreams. I can't pretend like it's not an alluring offer, but it's irrelevant. The factory isn't for sale.

I take a deep breath, and square my shoulders. "Mr. Roland, that's an incredibly generous offer, but I'm afraid I have to decline. My employees and their families rely on this factory and my loyalty is to them."

He pivots in his seat to lock eyes with his silent business partner, who gives him a firm nod.

"I understand," he says, turning back to me. "A million and a half then. Final offer."

One and a half million dollars. There's no hiding how tempted I am. I think of my father's medical bills, of the apartment I would be able to afford. Maybe an apartment a little closer to Chicago, a little closer to Barrett. And then I hear the familiar whir of the machines and the chatter of my employees, my second family, the ones I have to look out for above anything else.

"It's not for sale, Mr. Roland," I manage to sputter out, watching the beautiful apartment of my dreams slip out of reach.

"Fine. I see that you are in no place to make a deal today. That's fine. But my offer stands." He lifts his briefcase onto his lap and snaps it open, pulling a business card out between his middle and pointer finger like a Vegas blackjack dealer. "I'd encourage you to give it some serious thought. And while you're at it, do a little research on my company. I think you'll be impressed to see that your facility here would be in great hands. We have taken over factories much larger than this one in the past and seen wild success."

Roland extends the card across my desk and I reach out tentatively to take it. I flip the glossy, black card over and over in my hands, considering the cost of getting cards like these made. It's obvious that this guy is no joke—he's a serious businessman, and I ought to take his offer seriously, too.

"What are you looking to do with this facility, Mr. Roland?"

"That's of no importance to you, my dear," Roland says sharply. My jaw tightens at his use of the word 'dear.' "All you need to know is that you would be handsomely compensated."

"And what about the employees?"

"What about them?"

"My staff is my priority. I could never so much as consider selling without knowing for certain that the jobs of my staff would be kept intact. As well as their benefits and insurance policies. I'd need a direct role in the selection of all items pertaining to the employees."

"I had a feeling you would be looking for more information regarding that," he says, digging back into his briefcase and emerging with a manila folder. "So, I drafted up this contract. It's not written in stone, but it offers a good look at what the takeover might involve." He closes the briefcase with a decisive snap and slides the folder across the desk. I don't dare touch it, not wanting to show too much interest while he still has an eye on me.

"Give me a call whenever you're ready to talk business," Mr. Roland says, getting to his feet and extending his hand once again. "My attorney and I will be awaiting your response, Ava."

"Ms. Saunders."

"Yes. Ms. Saunders," he says flippantly, turning on his heels to leave. "Hold onto that card. You'll do the right thing."

The venom in his voice makes it sound more like a threat than a suggestion. I get up from my desk to see them out and close the door behind them, clicking the lock to ensure that I have complete privacy.

With a heavy breath, I settle back in at my desk and pull the summons papers back out of the drawer, setting them on the desk next to Mr. Roland's business card. I glance at the papers, then at the card. Each one is equally daunting. Still, it seems foolish to dismiss a $1.5 million offer when I'm staring down the barrel of this lawsuit. If my staff would be secure in their jobs, would it really be the worst thing in the world to let the company be in someone else's hands? But on the other hand, do I really want to sell out the business my father put decades of hard work into?

Between deciphering all this legal jargon and dealing with the new curveball of a potential buyout, there's no way I can navigate this without Barrett's help. He's a corporate lawyer, after all. Mom and Nick may have plenty of opinions on the subject, but Barrett has a little less bias and a lot more professional insight. Letting him advise me is the best move for the business.

And if it means I have to see him again, well, I certainly can't complain.

Chapter Twenty-four

Barrett

Busy streets stretch out toward the horizon beyond my window, as hundreds of cars and people leaving work push their way through traffic to get back home to their loved ones.

There's no reason for me to rush out into traffic, no one for me to go home to, so I usually wait for the rush hour to die down before leaving the office.

I glance at the email I haven't been able to respond to all day. It's from my step-sister Kimberly asking if I'm planning on bringing a plus one to the wedding. In a perfect world, I'd invite Ava. We'd sip champagne, and share a sweet kiss on the dance floor. Being near her just feels right, even if it'd be wrong in everyone else's eyes. I can't help how I feel.

But…how I feel hardly matters at the moment.

All I have to do to make partner is do my job; the one I busted my ass for all these years. Writing up contracts is second nature, seizing opportunity, capitalizing on weakness the second there's blood in the water—it's who I am.

But how can I do that now? If this was any other contract, I wouldn't even be questioning it.

The door to my office swings open and I straighten in my chair as Mr. Lyons walks in with a smile and his three-thousand-dollar suit. He doesn't smile much unless there's money involved.

"Barrett, how's that deal coming?" The expectation in his voice is clear; there's only one answer I can give.

"Good." I reflect the smile back, full of confidence. "One more signature and we'll have the whole thing locked down. A clean sale."

"I knew you were the man to take care of this." Lyons chuckles, satisfied with himself. "Since the day you started, I knew you had potential. All you needed was the right opportunity to prove yourself."

My stomach tightens in disapproval. "Thank you for giving me the opportunity then, sir."

"Of course. The partners have faith you'll see this through," he says, then steps back through my door.

When the latch shuts again, I sigh, then crack open the folder on my desk. All the paperwork is in order, every contract signed and certified except for one. I reach for the phone on my desk, only for it to buzz with a call before I can pick up.

"Mr. Wilson," the receptionist sounds a little surprised, and I can hear another woman insisting on something in the background, "there's an... Ava Saunders here to see you? She says it's urgent."

Ava is outside my office? "Go ahead and send her in."

Flipping the folder on my desk closed, I rise from my chair, ready to meet Ava at the door once she steps off the elevator.

It only takes a minute before I see her, but she's so harried that she nearly walks right past my office before I yank the door open and duck my head out. "Ava."

"Oh, Barrett!" She turns around, clutching a manila folder tight to her chest. "Sorry. The receptionist just said you were on this floor, but I wasn't sure where."

"Well, you found me." I gesture toward my desk. "Come on in."

She takes a seat in the chair across from mine, gathering herself together with a few deep breaths. I'm not sure I've ever seen her look so distraught before, but the reason is the contract she sets across my desk, fanning out the stack of papers like a handful of cards.

"Listen, I know I said I didn't need your help, but I was wrong." She bites her lip, fighting to keep her voice composed. "This is a trap. I can sense it. The people trying to buy the factory from me keep pushing and pushing, but won't give me any straight answers."

"Lawyers never give any straight answers," I say, but the joke lands flat on its face when her eyes glitter with unshed tears. My heart thumps hard in my chest, and I feel like someone's just punched me in the gut.

"I'm so scared. I think they're going to take the factory and everyone's jobs, and I don't know how to stop them. All the fine print is..." She runs her fingers across the tiny letters, where the full details of the agreement are hidden in subheadings and legalese. "I can't make any sense of it."

I know she can't. Not when I wrote out everything myself, crafting each demand the firm wanted in the most oblique terms. It would hold up in any court of law, but reads like nonsense to anyone who hasn't passed the bar.

Shit. Now that she's here, sitting right in front of me, I want to punch myself in the face.

A sharp knock on the door stops me from answering, and Mr. Roland walks in with a sly grin painted across his face. *What the fuck is he doing here?*

Completely ignoring the fact that I'm talking with someone, Roland walks right up to my desk, and knocks the rings on his hand against its smooth wooden surface.

"Barrett! The man of the hour." He jabs a thumb on the stack of contracts on my desk. "You wrote that agreement so tight an ant couldn't slip through it."

Ava's eyes lock on him, then jerk back over to me, panic flooding her pretty features.

Roland is still looking at me, grinning like a shark. "It's a good thing, too. We'll boot everyone working there out in two weeks and flip the property. The investors are already lining up."

"Roland." I grit my teeth, too on edge to even pretend to show him the respect I'm supposed to.

"Don't look so tense, son. You've got this." His attention falls on Ava finally, surprise playing out across his face. "Oh, you're in the middle of hashing things out with Ms. Saunders. I should get out of your way so she can sign off on the contract."

"Hashing out *what* with me?" she snaps, her face pale as she levels an accusatory glare at the folder sitting closed on my desk.

She reaches across to open the file, but I have to stop her, pulling it out of her reach. "Ava, you can't look at that. It belongs to the firm."

"It's the same contract they served me with, isn't it?" She gets up out of her seat, stuffing her copy of the contract back into its folder. "Your firm is representing these assholes? You want my factory. You set this whole thing up from the beginning just so you could get what you wanted? Well, fuck you, Barrett Wilson. Over my dead body."

"Roland, we need some privacy," I say hastily, and Mr. Roland steps out, confusion furrowing his gray brows. Once he's gone, I turn to Ava. "Please let me explain."

She moves toward the door, but I catch her by the arm, stopping her. The moment I touch her, she whirls around, defiance burning in her eyes. "Go to hell, Barrett. And get your hands off me."

She wrenches her arm out of my grasp, her face awash with so much hurt, it makes me physically ache. Because I never wanted this to happen, especially not like this.

"How dare you." Her voice is lower now but filled with just as much fury, almost a hiss. "Now it all makes sense."

"What makes sense?" I know she's angry, but I'm not following the leap of logic.

"You and me," she scoffs, shaking her head. "My whole life, you never showed any interest in me. Then you sweep on in and start helping everyone. Nick and my parents and—hitting on me like I was the hottest thing in town."

"Wait." I've wanted her since the beginning. Fuck. I've always wanted her. "That and this are *not* connected."

Her eyes narrow. "Sure, they're not. How am I supposed to believe anything you say?"

"It's true!" This sure as hell isn't the way I wanted to bring this up, but I'm not letting her leave here believing that I was trying to screw her over from day one. "The only reason I held back was because of your brother. I told you that."

"That's sure convenient. It didn't stop you in the end." She gives a half-hearted wave toward my window, hurt still shining in her eyes. "It didn't stop you from inviting me here, to Chicago, and using me."

"I wasn't using you." There's so much I want to explain, but giving her details of the firm's side of the deal would land my ass in hot water. "The last thing I wanted to do that weekend was go into work."

"But you did. And you've spent who knows how long building a case to take the factory out from under me." She glances down at the nameplate on my desk, at the business cards with the firm's name etched on them in black ink. "How could you represent these people, Barrett? They only care about money. They're going to take away hundreds of jobs and leave all those hardworking families behind."

"Ava, it's my job. I work for the clients that hire my firm, not the other way around." It's not like I want to fire everyone at the factory, but that's not my call. My responsibility is locking down the deal so it's all done legally. "They're going to make me partner for this."

She stares at me in disbelief, fingers holding onto the file folder so tight that the paper is starting to bend and warp. "So that's why. You saw the chance to get what you wanted, so screw everyone else, right?"

"I told you I had a chance to be partner and *you* encouraged me to take the case," I insist. "Your business was struggling to begin with. Everyone told you to sell and get the factory off your hands."

"You didn't." She sniffles, then rubs one hand over her face. "You said I was smart enough to make my own decisions."

"And this is the smart decision." As soon as I put two and two together, I did everything I could, from talking to the senior partner, to drafting heavy handed emails to make sure the company trying to buy the place offered her a fair price; that was the least I could do with my hands tied. "With that money, you can start any kind of business you want. Something you want to nurture, not holding onto your dad's old career."

"He gave up everything for that factory!" The volume fades from her voice as she draws in a ragged breath. "He almost died, Barrett. Just because you're heartless doesn't mean I'm going to be."

Heartless is the last thing I am right now. My pulse is like thunder in my chest, hammering with adrenaline. "So, what? You're going to sacrifice yourself to that place like he did? You're going to get sued for the accident and end up with nothing to show for it? How is that honoring your father's work?"

"How about your stepfather?" she accuses, voice sharp. "He worked at the factory before he passed away. Don't you care about that legacy at all?"

"My stepfather didn't give a shit about me." It's the truth, but some part of it still stings, the dull ache settling low in my gut. "We'd all be better off if that factory was in someone else's hands, instead of being chained to it."

She shakes her head, taking a step toward the door. Her voice comes out cool and confident. "I'm not going to stand here and listen to this anymore. I know whose side you're on now."

"It isn't like that." I'm gripping the edge of the doorframe so tight my knuckles feel like they're going to pop. I know the second she walks out of here, it's all over.

"I hate you." She looks me in the eyes as she says it, the anger in her gaze driving the words that much deeper. "I hate everything you've done. Don't even try and come back to see us in Indiana, because you're not welcome anymore."

Before I can respond, she storms out of my office, yanking the door shut behind her so hard the glass rattles. I'm left standing alone with that damn contract, wanting to flip my desk over and watch all the pages go flying. She knew exactly how to cut me to the bone, and she used everything in her arsenal to do it. The idea of her parents shutting the door in my face is almost more than I can take.

I was so close to getting everything I wanted. It felt even better than I dreamed, and it just walked out the door.

Chapter Twenty-five

Ava

I've been pacing the fifteen square feet of this lawyer's office for the past half an hour. I brought in any bit of paperwork that could possibly be relevant—the contract from Mr. Roland, the summons papers, and every printed off spreadsheet of the company's finances that I could find—and am waiting as patiently as I can while he scours every number and every word. There has to be something in there I'm missing, some unaccounted for fund or legal jargon I missed. Something that will help get me out of this parade of disasters.

The second I stormed out of Barrett's office in Chicago, I called Megan and proceeded to sob into the phone for almost the entire three-hour-drive home. She listened as I totally fell to pieces, relaying the entire train wreck of a day, then did what only best friends do: she completely saved my ass. Through some friend of a friend, she referred me to this lawyer who offered to help.

Sometimes, I think maybe Megan should be running my factory instead of me. She's so cool under pressure.

"There has to be a loophole, a get-around of some kind, right?" I chomp at the thumbnail on my left hand, the only nail yet to be chewed down since this meeting started. It's been years since I kicked my nail biting habit, but old habits tend to rear their ugly heads when the man you're completely in love with turns out to be the one running your company into the ground. I wave the thought of Barrett out of my head.

The lawyer, whose name has been pushed out of my mind by the million and one things I have to worry about, takes off his glasses and rubs his eyes. "Your hands are really tied here, Miss Saunders," he says sympathetically, shaking his head. "The plaintiff has an airtight case against you here, and you simply don't have the surplus to keep this business going in the midst of all this. It's economically more viable for you to sell."

"And what if I won't sell?"

The lawyer scoffs as if I were joking, but when he sees the serious look in my eyes, he clears his throat. "Well, then, you run the risk of going bankrupt in nine to twelve months, based on your current expenses. It's that simple."

My head is spinning at warp speed, the office around me blurring together. Nine to twelve months. In under a year, I could completely destroy the decades of work my father put into this company and come out on the other side with nothing to show for it. Or I could sell the business for a beautiful profit and demolish the livelihoods of dozens of men who practically raised me. Being caught between a rock and a hard place sounds comfortable compared to the spot I've been squeezed into.

"If you have any further questions or need additional legal counsel…" the lawyer starts, but trails off as I begin scooping up the paperwork off his desk with trembling hands.

"Th-thank you for your help. I have to go. I'll be in touch." Clutching the stack of paperwork to my chest, I half sprint, half stagger out the door. I can't listen to any more of this. I have a failing factory to get back to.

My foot is heavy on the gas pedal the whole drive back to work, easily exceeding the speed limit by a good fifteen miles per hour. What's the worst that happens, I get a speeding ticket? Just add it to the stack of paperwork. What's one more expense or run-in with the law at this point?

The money, the legal stuff, none of it matters nearly as much as my staff. I wonder how much they know? I haven't been transparent about everything with them, but with unfamiliar men in suits coming into the factory unannounced and my constant sneaking out, the warehouse has to be buzzing with talk of a takeover by now. And I wanted to be able to put an end to the rumors. Some deep gut feeling in me was so sure that I'd get to strut back into my office and tell Megan that this lawyer saved the day, that I didn't need Barrett's help or stupid Mr. Roland's money, that the solution was as clear as day and everything would work out just fine. But that deep gut feeling was wrong as hell. It would take more than a lawyer to help me now. It would take a friggin' miracle.

When I arrive back at the factory, the parking lot is surprisingly empty. Did I forget about a half day or something? My mind has been in at least fifty places at once lately; I wouldn't be surprised if today was a holiday and it totally slipped my mind. I check my phone for the time—it's only 3:30, a little early for everyone to have already called it a day. I enter through the side door to avoid making eye contact with any lingering employees and find Megan sitting at my desk, waiting to be relieved of her duties. I feel the slightest bit relieved when I see her, and count my blessings that I have a friend good enough to take time away from her job to come and look over the plant while I was away.

"Is it a holiday that I forgot about?" The usual whir of the machines is missing. Looking past Nat and through the window into the warehouse, the place is a ghost town other than the few guys cleaning and locking up.

"I wish," she says. "How'd things go with the lawyer?"

"About as badly as you could dream up. We're screwed," I sigh, plopping all the paperwork back down on my desk. "Well, I'm screwed. You can head out if you want. Looks like everyone else has," I say, gesturing toward the window to the warehouse.

"Well, I hate to be the one to tell you that the bad news doesn't end there. I had to send everyone home,

Ava." She announces it as if it were news, waiting for my surprised reaction like I'm not staring into the nearly empty warehouse through the window behind her.

"I don't understand? If that engine fell again, I swear to God."

"No, the engine is fine. The problem is everything else. Some guy came by while you were gone." She picks up a piece of paper and stares at it with intense focus, avoiding eye contact with me. "An inspector from the Occupational Safety and Health Administration."

Shit.

"The Mark incident must have been reported to them and I was required by the state to let him survey the place," she explains, finally looking up at me with sympathetic eyes. "And I guess he didn't like what he found. He commanded that the place be shut down effective immediately for lack of compliance with safety regulations."

"Which safety regulations?"

She nervously hands over the document she's been holding. The whole page is completely marked up with red ink and highlighter, documenting every loose screw and dusty vent in the building. There has to be at least two dozen violations here. How did I not know about any of these? Factories may not be my area of expertise, but I'm not dumb. Was I so caught up in my Barrett fantasies that I didn't manage to notice that this factory I've been running is a giant mess?

"He said once all the highlighted violations were corrected that they would come back," Megan says, as if it's supposed to offer me any solace. "They're willing to reassess the property to determine whether or not you can reopen your doors. But until then, the factory has to stay closed, Ava. I'm so sorry."

"So, I'm just shut down?" I snap, the tears already building in my eyes. "I'm done? Just like that?" My voice has escalated to a yell, but I don't care. Let the handful of employees left in the warehouse hear me. It's not any secret that things are falling apart.

"There's still hope," she offers, getting up from behind my desk to try to calm me down.

"Where? Where is there hope?" My throat twists and tightens as tears start to spill down my cheeks in quiet rivers. "I don't think I saw a line item in the budget for hope."

"I'm just trying to help." She puts up her hands in defense and takes a step back from me. I'm derailing and she's taking the brunt of it, but I can't hold myself together. How could so many disasters hit back to back to back?

There's a knock on the door— probably one of the few guys still on site coming to find out if he needs to start looking for a new job. I try to deep breathe so I can preserve some of my dignity in front of my employees, but when the door creaks open, the familiar grating voice that greets me belongs to no employee of mine.

"Ava, I hope I'm not interrupting."

I snap my head around to meet Roland's beady eyes as he slithers into the room.

His timing is impeccable.

"I just thought I might swing by before your end of day...although it looks like maybe everyone's called it quitting time already." His greasy smirk replaces my sadness with pure anger. How dare he show up again, completely unannounced.

"What do you want, Roland?" I bark.

"I just wanted to stop in and see if you were ready to sign that agreement," he says it as though it were some innocent suggestion. Could he know about the health inspector, or is this just some crazy coincidence? Either way, I'm still not going down without a fight.

"Over my dead body, Roland." My voice wobbles as I say it, but I've never been more secure in my stance. I'd sooner let this company land in the dumpster before laying it in Roland's hands.

The few lingering workers wander into the doorframe, drawn to the commotion.

"Well, no matter," he says, waving me off and turning to address what's left of my staff. "Gentleman, I hope you'll spread word to the rest of the employees that Roland Enterprises will be hosting a meeting this coming Saturday in our main conference room. An open panel, if you will. I hope you'll all attend to hear what I have to say about the future of this business and our intentions." The men shoot me "we're so sorry" looks, but give Roland a nod. Clearly this is coming as no surprise to them.

"I'd just like to handle things in a reasonable, professional manner," Roland says, pivoting back to address me. "I don't want anyone getting laid off any more than you do."

That is such bullshit. I heard what he said in Barrett's office.

Chapter Twenty-six

Barrett

Any time I forget why I want to move up and become a partner at the firm, I'm reminded of Mr. Lyons' office. Any interior designer would start drooling the second they got a look at the place—from the desk to the leather chairs to the bookshelf lined with legal books filled with historic cases, all the furniture sleek and black. Not a nick or a smudge on anything. He's got the nicest office of anyone in the firm, maybe of anyone on this city block, and the man knows it.

Sometimes, I feel like he calls people in for meetings just so that they can ogle the place. The second you walk in the view is enough to knock you down a peg—the entirely glass walls look out over the water taxis and barges headed down the Chicago River. Not that Mr. Lyons gets to enjoy that view—his desk faces away from the windows, leaving whatever poor sad sack he's meeting with to squint into the sun for the full duration of the meeting. Today, that poor sad sack is me.

An email from the boss popped up in my inbox last night asking me to be here at 11 am sharp. I wasn't planning on coming in on a Saturday when I could possibly work from home, but whatever Lyons says goes. So, I left my apartment early not wanting to chance my luck with the weekend traffic. Luckily, I'm on and off the road before any of the tourists start driving into the city. I make it to the office with enough time to grab a coffee before I settle into the leather chair that faces Mr. Lyons' desk.

"Good morning, Barrett. You're here early." There is no surprise in his voice; he's simply stating a fact.

"Early is on time and on time is late, just like you always say, Mr. Lyons."

I can almost detect a smile creeping onto his face as he thumbs leisurely through his portfolio, leaving me in anticipation as to what he needs me for that couldn't wait until Monday.

"Mr. Roland and I spoke at length last night of the importance of your attendance at tonight's meeting with the factory staff," he says, not bothering to look up from his paperwork. "Having grown up in that town, we feel that your word on the takeover may be more influential than Roland's. You'll be a more familiar face, far more trustworthy. And if that stubborn girl running the factory is ever going to budge on signing the place over, we'll need her whole staff on our side."

That stubborn girl?

My stomach twists and tightens, and my hands ball into fists as I squeeze the armrests of the chair. Of all the reasons for calling me into work on a Saturday morning, this is certainly the worst. I'm filled with equal parts dread and rage. I'd rather draft and redraft a hundred new merger agreements while naked and being roasted over a fire than have to stand in front of Ava while I blatantly lie to her whole staff.

"You're a persuasive man, Barrett." He finally closes his portfolio of paperwork and graces me with eye contact. "And these Indiana factory men can relate to you. You're one of them." He glances over my suit and tie then adds, "At least, you used to be. They know you. I'm sure you'll have no trouble getting them on board, as long as you keep it vague about the terms and conditions of the agreement."

"Is there any possibility of modifying that agreement?" I know it's a long shot, but it's worth a try. If I'm as persuasive as Mr. Lyons thinks I am, maybe I can pull this off. "I've been giving a lot of thought to the contract and what would be the most beneficial for all parties involved. If Roland Enterprises would be willing to keep the facility running, we could save a lot of jobs in this community. Roland could always use the factory space. Maybe we could organize an emergency meeting with Mr. Roland before he meets with the factory staff tonight. Do a bit of revising."

Mr. Lyons shoots me his patented over-the-glasses look and the vein in his forehead throbs. I guess that's a no.

"Barrett, you wrote the damn agreement yourself. If this was a concern of yours, you should've voiced it a long time ago or you should have excused yourself for conflicts of interest. Roland Enterprises wants that space for a storage warehouse. End of discussion."

"But-"

"No buts about it." Mr. Lyons pushes himself out of his chair and walks along the edge of his office, taking in the view outside. "Need I remind you what you stand to gain here? The corner office, your name on the door, a major salary increase. That's just the start of things for you. This is a lot bigger for you than one silly factory. This is the future of your career." He snaps back around to face me, his arms folded tightly over his chest. "Are you going or not?"

Why does he phrase it as if I really have an option?

"I'll be there."

The corner of his mouth twitches into a smile. Returning to his chair, he brings his attention back to the paperwork on his desk.

"That's what I thought," he says offhandedly. "You might use that three hours in the car to work on your speech. Good luck. I'll expect a summary of the meeting in my inbox by tomorrow morning."

I wait another moment to ensure Mr. Lyons is done with me, but he shows no intention of looking back up from his paperwork, so I take that as my cue to head back to my car.

Had I been given any advanced notice about this, I might have been able to drive out last night, try to meet up with Ava and patch things up a bit before tonight's shit show, but instead I've got five hours until the meeting, and not the faintest clue what I'm going to say to these people, or to Ava. How do I tell her that I love her and then destroy her company in the same breath?

Fuck.

I love her. So damn much.

I guess I knew, but I hadn't admitted it to myself yet. I love her, and I'm about to let her down again.

Tourist traffic has started up, so I sit bumper to bumper with everyone else in the city for a solid hour before I make it home. That leaves me with only four hours and still no plan. Shit.

I'm not sure if it's the right thing to do, but before I even get out of my car, I call Nick. I've got to talk this through with somebody and there's no point in keeping secrets from him anymore. He agrees to hop in his car and head over, which should get him to my apartment in thirty minutes. I spend that whole half hour pacing, looking for any way out of all of this that doesn't end in me losing my job, Ava, or my best friend…or worse yet, all three.

By the time Nick buzzes up, I've tried out over a dozen different ways of bending the truth, but I know I can't lie to him any better than I can lie to these guys at the meeting tonight.

I may get decked for it, but I'm better off just manning up and shooting him straight. Nick knocks on the door a few times to be polite, but as usual, he walks right in once he realizes it's unlocked.

"Hey, man, are you okay?" he asks as he taps the snow off his boots. "You sounded weird on the phone." When I shrug him off, he throws his keys on the counter and plops himself onto the couch.

It never takes much of an invitation for Nick to make himself at home. I've got half a mind to get a beer or two in him before I break the news, but we're short on time. Might as well get right to it.

"I've got to talk to you about something." I go back to pacing the living room, not sure if I have the balls to look him in the eye. "You're not going to like it, and I know that I'm probably going to lose you as a friend because of this. And that really sucks. But I'm going to say it anyway."

"Barrett, chill out. We've been friends for pretty much our whole lives. It would take a hell of a lot to screw that up."

I plant my feet and take a deep breath. *Here comes a hell of a lot.*

"I love you like a brother, man. You know that. But also...I love your sister."

Nick rolls his eyes, relaxing back into the couch. "That's it? So, what? She's my sister, I hope you'd care about her."

"No, I mean I love her. I'm in love with Ava. And I want to be with her."

His eyes widen and lock onto mine. "Are...are you joking?"

"No."

I can practically watch the gears in his head turn as he starts piecing things together—the moments of tension he interrupted at his parents' house, the times Ava and I would disappear together, everything.

"So, you mean when you said you couldn't hang out a couple of weeks ago, that chick that you had here in the apartment...was that Ava?"

Shit. Maybe I should lie and say it was someone else, pretend that nothing physical has happened between me and Ava. I don't want to show up to this meeting tonight with a black eye.

"Barrett. Answer me. Was she here?"

I shouldn't have paused for that long. If I lied now, no way he would believe me. *Brace yourself, Barrett.*

"Yes, she spent the weekend here with me."

"Son of a bitch." Nick leaps off the couch and lunges at me and I duck out of the way. He takes a step back, cooling down and pulling himself together as he paces the room. "My goddamn sister, you son of a bitch," he mutters through his teeth. "The one damn thing that should have been off-limits and you can't keep your dick in your pants."

"I'm sorry, Nick, but it wasn't like that." Actually, that's exactly how this started, when she caught me coming out of the shower...but he doesn't need to know that. "I've had a crush on her for a while now. Years. And seeing her again...things just kind of clicked. I can't help how I feel. If I could control it, I would. Believe me. The last thing I want to do is fuck up our friendship."

He stops dead in his tracks, then turns back to me, his squinty eyes sizing me up. "Really? You're telling me if you could control it, if you could turn on a dime and suddenly *not* love my sister, you would?"

He's got me there.

"No. No, I wouldn't," I admit. "You're right. I wouldn't give her up."

He shakes his head and takes his spot on the couch again. "Then I guess it must be something real."

Things have calmed down enough that I decide to test my luck and grab a seat on the couch next to him. He doesn't immediately reach over and strangle me, which seems like a good sign.

"So, how many times do you have to knee me in the balls until we're even?" I'm only half joking, but it gets a smirk out of Nick.

"You've got to deal with something that hurts way worse, man. The wrath of Ava. She's never going get over the fact that you're the ringleader in this whole takeover business. I've never seen her this furious."

"Has she said anything about me?"

Nick snorts. "How the hell would I know, she hasn't spoken a word to me since I told her she'd be better off selling."

"You told her I told you to sell?"

Nick wags a finger at me like he's scolding a dog. "Don't turn this on me. You're the one who's been getting it on with my sister behind my back."

"I'm not getting it on with her, Nick. I love her."

"Shit, that sounds so goddamn weird." He makes a face, and shakes his head like he's trying to clear a visual image.

"Well then, this next part is going to sound even weirder." I glance at my watch—three hours until the meeting, and it's at least a three-hour drive. *Fuck.* "Help me get your sister back?"

Holding Nick's coat out in front of me as a peace offering, I watch him think it over. The whole thing is crazy, and with the news I just dropped on him, I don't expect him to help me, but twenty-plus years of friendship has to mean something, right?

He squeezes his eyes shut and takes in a long breath, then reaches out to take his coat. "Alright, let's do it. I hope you've got one hell of a plan."

"I don't." I give him a wicked grin and fastball him his keys. "But just like with every game we ever played, we'll think on our feet and I'll make one up on the way there."

Chapter Twenty-seven

Ava

As terrified as I am for the meeting with Roland and my staff tonight, there's a much tougher, infinitely more nerve-wracking meeting I have to get through first. The one with my dad.

How do I go about telling my father that, after he handed his life's work over to me, I've let it fall to pieces? There's no way he can be totally blindsided—he ran the factory for decades, after all. He knows the budgets back and forth, and as much as I have tried to hide my stress, I know he's seen me practically pulling my hair out over every new disaster.

Somehow, we've made it this far without having to have a real discussion about the state of things at the plant. But there's no avoiding it anymore. As I descend the stairs to the den, I repeat over and over again in my head that Dad gave me the factory for a reason—I'm smart and I'm strong. Still, I don't know a girl in the world with the kind of strength to look her dad in the eye and admit she's let him down.

"Daddy? Can I talk to you?"

He's lounging in his usual spot, smack dab in the middle of the couch, a basketball game on the TV. When he hears my voice, he doesn't so much as turn, just slides over and pats the cushion next to him.

We sit there side by side and watch the game for a few minutes as I try to figure out where I should even begin. Maybe I should've practiced in front of a mirror first or written a script. When the ref calls a time out, Dad leans toward the coffee table and grabs the remote, muting the sounds of sportscasters and sneaker squeaks.

"Big meeting tonight, huh?" he says, eyes still on the muted game.

"How do you know that?"

"I may not be running the plant anymore, but it's not like the fellas and I don't talk."

Shit, I hadn't even thought about the fact that Dad might already know more than I do about what's going on.

"If you knew, then why haven't you said anything to me?"

Dad sighs, leaning back into the couch. When he finally turns and looks at me, I brace myself for anger, at least frustration, but instead, his eyes are kind. He's calm as ever.

"It's not my company anymore, Ava. It's yours. And I know you've got it under control."

It's my turn to sigh. "It sure doesn't feel like it right now, Dad. I think this might be it for the plant. I think I'm going to lose it."

Dad lets the silence hang in the air for a good long while. I look down at my fingernails, but I have nothing left to bite at, the weeks of worry and indecision have taken their toll on my poor nails. When I look back up at Dad, I'm surprised to find him smiling. It's a soft, sad smile, but a smile, nonetheless.

"I'm proud of you, kid," he says, his tone warm and certain. "You've done good."

Is he losing his hearing? How could he possibly be proud of me? I search his eyes for any sign that he might be kidding, but he seems sincere.

"You don't have to lie to me, Dad," I say, picking at my nails as a replacement anxious habit. "I've done anything but good. I've single-handedly run everything you built straight into the ground."

"The guys at the plant might surprise you," he suggests with a shrug. "They've surprised me before. This is more about them than it is about you. The whole business is about them. I've told you that since day one. Don't forget that."

"Of course not. I've never forgotten that. But even if I walk into that meeting with my head held high, everyone knows I'm going to walk out defeated."

"That might be true, it might not be. But you don't know until you get in there and give it the rest of what you've got."

"I'm not sure how much I've got left."

"You've still got some fight in you." He slugs me lightly on the arm, like a coach preparing his pinch hitter to take the plate. "You know how I know?"

A knowing smile creeps across my face. "How do you know, Dad?"

"Because you take after me, sweetie. That's how."

* * *

The headquarters of Roland Enterprises look more like a spaceship than an office. The massive silver building towers over every structure in the area. Its giant windows and huge silver doors feel out of place in rural Indiana. When I walk through the extra tall automatic doors, there's no front desk, no attendant to greet me, only a line of touch screen kiosks showing a map through this enormous building.

Toto, I don't think we're at the factory anymore. Lucky for me, the conference room is just down the hall from the big icon on the map that says, "You are here," so I won't have to get too deep into this place and run the risk of getting lost. It also means that, if necessary, I can make a quick escape back to my car if the meeting is a total disaster.

When I turn down the hall, I can hear the murmuring of my employees coming from a distance. Just hearing their voices brings a more comfortable familiarity to this place. I follow their voices to a set of swinging grey doors that lead to the site of this evening's main event.

The conference room has been arranged so that the chairs are in rows facing a podium at the front of the room, making it feel more like a press conference than a meeting. How very like Roland to set up the room to put himself front and center, standing over everyone else. Most of the guys have shown up, filling the room with nervous energy and small talk about sports, the weather, anything but the issue at hand. Time to get this group focused.

I take a deep breath, and remember Dad's pep talk. Then I head straight to the front of the room, and all of the conversation dies down and a sea of anxious faces turns to look at me.

"Hey, guys, can we chat really quick before things get started?"

It stays quiet, and my belly fills with nerves.

You can do this, Ava.

I consider the podium, but instead choose a chair near the front of the room and turn it so I'm facing my staff. We're all on the same level here.

"In the short time I've been in charge of this factory, a lot has happened that I admit I have not always handled correctly. I was trying to fix everything but not very good about asking for help when I needed it. When we needed it. And for that, I can't apologize enough."

I pause to glance up at the doors. No sign of Roland yet. Might as well keep going.

"There's a lot that I have to learn from all of you about this factory, and if you are willing to give me that chance, I would be honored to have you teach me. This business has been around for a long time, and in that time it has grown so much. I know we have more growing to do, and I want to take on that challenge. You know how much I care about this company, and how much I care about each and every one of you and your families. I have since I was a little girl. My father built something truly incredible here, a real family. I ask you all to find it within you not to give up on our family just yet."

"Truly inspiring, Ava." The doors swing open and Roland struts into the room, his beady eyes boring into me. "Now, if we might get down to the facts." His condescending tone makes me feel like a student who has been misbehaving in class while the teacher was gone, but I refuse to make myself small in front of him. I have to stand my ground and summon that fight I have still in me. This one's for you, Dad.

As Roland approaches the podium, I swivel my chair back to its original position and walk to the front of the room, standing just to the left of him.

"What are you doing?" he hisses through his teeth.

"This is my company. Since you seem to have forgotten a podium for me, I'll be standing up here next to you so that we can both address my staff, if that's quite alright."

He inhales slowly, then lets out a punctuated breath. "Fine. It doesn't make a difference where you stand." After clearing his throat a thin smile spreads across his face as he turns to face the crowd.

"Thank you all for coming today, gentleman," he begins, his voice dripping with a phony friendliness. "I'm deeply excited to discuss the potential of Roland Enterprises taking over your company. We are prepared to buy out the factory from Ava and transfer power within the next month, at which point I would hire you all on to help renovate the factory, no loss of jobs. We would move toward an automated system, which you would help to run behind the scenes."

The doors swing open again and Barrett and Nick saunter in, leaving me to dig what's left of my fingernails into my palms to keep from screaming. The nerve of them to show up to this meeting. Why are they here? To say, "I told you so" and rub salt in my wounds? So, Barrett can flaunt his betrayal in my face? And Nick can encourage the factory workers to side with Roland?

They take seats in the back, and I pretend not to notice them, focusing instead on whatever drivel Roland is spewing as he fields questions from the crowd. Luckily, the men are giving him looks of uncertainty. I knew they wouldn't buy into this. Any factory employee who hears the word automation knows what that means—you won't need as many humans to run a facility that's automated.

"Maybe it would help to hear this from someone who understands you a bit better than I do, one of your own. Barrett, didn't you grow up in the area?"

I refuse to give Barrett the satisfaction of looking at him, but I can see him nodding out of the corner of my eye.

"Would you mind telling these fine gentlemen about what this takeover could provide for them and their community?" Roland gestures at the podium, inviting Barrett to take the reins.

For fuck's sake. I feel like I'm going to hurl.

After everything we shared together, his betrayal hurts ten thousand times more than losing the company from right out under me.

I can feel Barrett's piercing gaze on me as he steps up to the front of the room, but I still refuse to look him in the eye. How could he? It's one thing just to have the guts to come to this meeting, but to speak? To put the final nail in the coffin of my family's business? I wish I could disappear. That, or strangle him.

Roland steps out of the way, taking a seat to allow Barrett to take the stand.

"It's true, Mr. Roland offers a lot of great ideas for this factory," he begins. Tears spring to my eyes and I frantically try to blink them back. The least I can do is go down with a little grace.

Deep breaths.

"Well, a lot of good ideas about turning it into a storage facility that is."

What?

"Roland Enterprises plans to automate the factory completely within the year this is true, but the automation will not be to assist you in doing your jobs. It will be to turn the building into a storage warehouse. No production, nothing but back stock and machines that sort the inventory, eliminating all of your jobs in a year's time."

Roland jumps to his feet in protest. "Barrett, that is quite enough. Ava, take the stand from Barrett, it's your turn to speak."

"You will address her as Miss Saunders, show some respect, Roland. Now, why don't you take your seat while I break down the fine print for these gentlemen?"

Roland's jaw tightens, his eyes wide and manic. "I don't think you want to do that, Barrett."

Barrett turns to me, sees the shock in my eyes, and offers me a sweet, apologetic smile. "Oh, I know I do, Roland." He gives me a wink, then squares his shoulders with the podium again, looking out over the crowd and launching into his speech.

"The Roland Enterprises takeover would be an excellent move for Mr. Roland here, but the impact on the staff and the community overall would be overwhelmingly negative." I peek over to check if he's reading this off of something, but the podium is empty. He's doing this off the cuff.

"I am confident in saying that Ms. Saunders is more than capable of running this plant, but she cannot do it without all of you. In fact, if the company shifted some of you into more management-based roles, allowing you to offer more insight from a mechanical standpoint, I suspect the factory could increase its efficiency and its profits in no time at all. All it would take is some legal help to restructure the company."

My eyes are welling up with tears again, but this time, they're tears of absolute joy and disbelief. This seems too good to be true, like just another Barrett fantasy, but a quick pinch of my arm ensures me I'm not dreaming. Barrett Wilson, teen heartthrob turned corporate lawyer, is abandoning his own client to side with me. No doubt losing his job and his accelerated partner track.

"Ava has an excellent business model," Barrett goes on. "As a corporate lawyer, I can speak to the fact that there are few companies left that really prioritize their employees. You're lucky to have a boss like her. And if you have a good thing…" He pivots back to me, his intense blue eyes locking with mine. "You shouldn't let it go."

From the back of the crowd comes one slow clap, then another, until the whole staff is on their feet applauding Barrett's speech, calling out "well said!" and "hell yeah!" When I spot Nick standing and clapping with the best of them, the tears spill over onto my cheeks. I guess Dad was right. Sometimes, people can surprise you.

The moment is next to perfect until Roland leaps up, silencing the crowd with a loud "Wait, wait, wait!"

"This is ridiculous!" Roland barks. "Company restructuring? There isn't a firm on Earth that this company could afford with their current deficit."

"I'm sure they can find someone to do the work pro bono," Barrett says with a smirk, waving Roland's criticism out of the air. "In fact," he says, glancing at me over his shoulder, "I think I know just the guy."

Chapter Twenty-eight

Barrett

"You got a lot of nerve, Barrett."

Mr. Roland stomps up to the podium, cell phone in one hand and briefcase in the other. His head looks like an overripe tomato. I knew I'd royally fuck myself and piss a client off someday, I just didn't think I'd be so happy about it.

"You're finished," he hisses, stretching one arm over the podium to shove his phone in my face. My boss' name glows bright on the screen above the ticking clock indicating the length of the call. "I've had the senior partner on the line from the second you went off the rails up there. Maybe you'd like to tell him about your little eruption."

I snatch the phone out of Roland's hand and press it up to my ear. "Hello?" Mr. Lyons' gruff voice is almost entirely drowned out by the chaos of the room, all the factory guys high fiving and rushing Ava to congratulate her. I don't blame them. I'd be doing the same thing if this asshole hadn't stopped me first. I cup my hand over my other ear to quiet the room a bit. "Sorry, could you say that again?"

"I said what the hell was that little speech, Barrett?" He's yelling now, which I actually appreciate since it makes him easier to hear. "You just ruined this firm's name. And for what?"

"The firm ruined its own name by its complete lack of ethics," I explain coolly. "Which is why I won't be working for you anymore."

"You sure as hell won't!" he barks. "You're fired!"

"That's not possible, sir." I lock eyes with Roland, directing my words at him just as much as my boss. "Because if you were listening, I just quit." The smug look on Roland's face fades into a snarl. Did he really think he could win that easily?

"You're useless without the firm," Mr. Lyons hisses, but we both know that's a lie. With my experience, I can find work almost anywhere.

"If you get any inquiries from potential small business clients, feel free to send them in the direction of my new firm, which I will be establishing here in Indiana. I'd be happy to work with them." I press the button to end the call. No way in hell is that jerk getting the last word. I take the liberty of deleting my number from Roland's phone before sliding it across the podium to him.

"You're a joke, Barrett," Roland sputters. "You know as well as I do that you can't keep this plant open. There's hardly a factory in the country that's still paying employees instead of making the switch to an automated solution. All you're doing is buying time until she has to eventually sell that dump."

"You may be right." A look of pleasant surprise washes over Roland's features, but it doesn't last long. "Maybe she'll have to sell next year, or even next month. But until then, I'm going to be here helping her keep it open as long as we can. And if it comes to the point of selling, I'll be there to make sure the business ends up in the hands of someone who actually cares. Which I guess eliminates you, doesn't it?"

Roland's tomato face ripens two shades of red. I'm kind of surprised he hasn't had an aneurysm. "Everyone needs to get out of our building immediately!" he screeches over the crowd, but no one seems to be bothered or even notice. He marches out of the conference room with a huff, slamming the door behind him, although I don't even hear it shut over all the whooping and hollering from the guys as he leaves.

Now that he's gone, I can get back to the real reason why I'm here.

Ava.

She's standing at the side of the room, surrounded by of a long line of employees, fielding questions, compliments, and handshakes while she thanks them for their loyalty through this crazy process.

She's absolutely glowing, happier than I've ever seen her, and I can't help but crack a smile knowing I played a part in making that happen. I join the back of the line of admirers to wait my turn for her attention, but the guy in front of me elbows the guy in front of him and suddenly they're letting me cut to the front. Looks like I've got a room full of wingmen.

I don't even know where to begin, so when Ava and I are finally face to face, all I can manage is "Hey."

"Hey." She smiles, tucking her hair behind her ear. Why is it that defending her in front of a room full of people was so easy, but just looking her in the eye is so hard? I gather all my confidence in a deep breath and as I exhale, the apology starts spilling out of me.

"I am so, so sorry, Ava. I can't apologize enough. You don't have to forgive me now, I know I don't deserve it. But I'm going to work as hard as I can to earn it. I-"

She doesn't let me finish my thought, throwing her arms around my neck and pressing her mouth against mine in a wild kiss that almost knocks me back.

When she pulls back, she slaps a hand over her mouth, her eyes darting around the room in a frenzy. For a second, I try to figure out what's wrong. It's not like any of the guys from the factory are going to care if their boss is kissing the lawyer. Who cares?

"Nick, I'm so sorry," she says, voice breathless and shaky.

Oh, that's who.

Fuck.

I pivot over my shoulder and find myself toe to toe with Nick. He's making a scrunched-up face of disgust like he just smelled something rotten, or did a vodka shot and doesn't have a chaser to follow it up with.

"Are you mad?" Ava peers timidly over my shoulder, using me as a human shield against her brother. Nick considers it for a second, but his sour face eventually relaxes a bit as he shakes his head.

"Less mad than I am just weirded out," he says with a shudder. "I'm just glad I knew before I saw you guys all over each other. Barrett already told me earlier that he loves you."

If looks could kill, the glare I give Nick would, at the very least, land him in the emergency room.

"Thanks a lot, man. Kind of wanted to tell her that part myself."

Nick shrugs apologetically and backs up a bit, giving us what little bit of privacy this busy conference room has to offer.

"You love me?" There are tears in her eyes.

I can barely breathe with the way she's looking at me. This isn't exactly how I pictured this moment with Ava—in a corporate conference room of the enemy with her brother standing five feet away. But the secret's out now, so all I can do is play up whatever small amount of romance the situation can offer. I smile and she bites her lip in that way that drives me absolutely wild.

"How could I not?"

Her eyes flash bright as she grabs me by the lapels of my jacket, pressing up onto her tippy toes to take my lower lip between hers. She's tender and slow, even as her staff cheers. I can feel her smiling through the kiss until the moment she pulls away.

"I love you, too, Barrett."

As her words wash through me, so does a strong sense of calm. I shouldn't feel this good—I just lost my job, yet I've never felt better.

"Then that settles it. I'm moving to Indiana to be close to you." Ava furrows her brow, but I keep talking through her concern, wrapping my arms around her waist.

It feels like centuries since I've held her; now that I have her back, there's no way I'm letting go. "And before you say anything, I don't want you to worry, I'm not giving anything up by leaving Chicago. Just a bunch of eighty-hour weeks working for someone else. Instead, I'll open my own private practice here where I'll be able to make time for what really matters."

The worry in her eyes doesn't go away like I'd hoped it would. Instead, she shimmies out of my arms with a groan. "You don't have to do that, Barrett," she says under her breath so that her staff can't hear. "Half of what I said was bravado anyway. It's not in the budget for me to get the factory back up to safety codes. We're going to have to stay shut down."

"Hey, now." I tilt her chin up with two fingers so that her gaze meets mine. "I wouldn't worry so much about that. I might know a guy who recently put his apartment in the city on the market. There's a lot of money to be had there. And come to think of it, he owes you big time."

The life re-enters Ava's eyes, her lips spreading into a tight smile. "I can't believe you did that for me," she murmurs tenderly.

"I did that for us, Ava."

She blushes as I offer her my hand, and it feels so right when I lace our fingers together. I nod my chin toward the door. "You ready to get out of here?"

There's no reason to stay in this corporate wasteland any longer. After all, we have a lot of company restructuring work to do. She squeezes my hand and gives me a smile of approval, but then turns away and clears her throat before she addresses her staff one more time.

"We'll meet first thing on Monday to discuss our new business plan, all right?" She's met with a blend of "Yes, ma'am!" and "Aye-aye!" As we walk out the doors of Roland Enterprises and into the parking lot, the whole team follows behind us.

"See? You're a great leader already," I whisper to her, which elicits a giggle in response. I carpooled with Nick on the way from Chicago, but it seems like the obvious choice to ride with Ava now. I slide into the passenger seat and buckle in. I'd offer to drive, but Lord knows how much she loves to be in control.

"Mind if we go back to your place one last time?" she suggests. "It might be a bit more private." She pauses, then adds, "You know, for planning the restructuring." Her cheeks turn rose pink. God, she's adorable.

"My place sounds great," I say, laying a gentle kiss on one of her blushing cheeks as she turns the ignition and the car rumbles to life.

"Although, once my apartment sells, any chance your mom might be able to accommodate me on her couch again until I lock down a new place?"

Ava laughs as she peels out of the parking lot, heading straight for the highway without needing directions from me.

"I'm sure we'd all be happy to have you."

Epilogue

Ava

Indiana winters can feel practically endless, but I stand by the fact that the summers make it all worth it. Summer is winding down and it's a perfect seventy-eight degrees, not a cloud in the sky above our little backyard barbecue.

From the moment the realtor showed us this two-story blue house on the end of the cul-de-sac, with its updated kitchen and huge backyard, I knew Barrett and I had to have it. I could perfectly envision hosting parties on the red brick patio and roasting marshmallows over the stone fire pit on a fall night.

We signed the paperwork and closed on the place within a month of our first walk-through. The location is perfect, too, it's almost the exact midpoint between the factory and the office Barrett is renting for his new law firm, and with Mom and Dad's place only a few miles down the road, we get plenty of opportunities to have the whole family over.

No Mom and Dad today, though. Just Nick and Dana for a double date to celebrate finally being moved in. The two of them have been practically inseparable since the day Nick ditched Barrett and me to go on a date with her, leaving us to cover party supply shopping on our own. With how things turned out, of course, I'm happy that he did.

Barrett has been manning the grill all afternoon. Meanwhile, I've taken on the hard labor of snacking on potato chips and dancing to the radio, so I've also been on beverage duty, as well. I pop the top off of two long neck bottles, one for him and one for me.

"Working awfully hard there. You ready for another?" I wander closer to Barrett, and he accepts the beverage, squeezing my backside with his other hand. I raise one brow at him in warning. "Behave."

He shrugs, a smile on his full mouth. "Your ass looks nice in those shorts."

As I take a swig, I can't help but notice the way the sunlight hits my ring. It's been about a month since

Barrett and I said, "I do" but I think it would take several lifetimes for me to get over how beautiful this ring is.

I knew he could afford a nice-sized rock with how well business has gone at his practice, but this enormous princess cut diamond blew all of my expectations out of the water. Still, he could've proposed with the metal ring from a can of corn and I would've said yes.

"Staring again?" Barrett smiles coyly and squeezes my side with the hand that isn't gripping the spatula. He wraps his arm around my waist and pulls me tight against him, kissing me and flipping a burger at the same time. The man is nothing if not talented.

"Get a room, you two," Nick calls from the hammock, although he has Dana nuzzled up in the crook of his arm. I also happen to know that he's got a ring in his pocket, as if today wasn't already perfect enough.

"We're married dude, remember? You're going to have to be okay with it." Barrett pulls me in close before dipping me back into a much longer, deeper kiss, making a show of it just to get on Nick's nerves.

"Just because I'm okay with it doesn't mean I'm ever gonna get used to it." Nick sits up and grabs his beer off the ground, smiling while he takes a sip.

"Well, maybe keep throwing those beers back until you *are* used to it," Barrett teases, turning off the grill. "Now come and grab some food while it's still hot."

I survey the spread we've laid out across the picnic table—chicken, burgers, corn on the cob, potato salad, sliced watermelon, and a giant red cooler filled to the brim with icy cold drinks. It's the perfect summer picnic and it makes me fall in love with our little backyard even more. Once Dana and Nick have pulled themselves off of each other, I distribute paper plates, which everyone immediately starts piling high with food.

"Do the guys have off Labor Day this year?" Nick asks as he grabs a slice of watermelon.

"Of course. I'm not a monster. And with the way things have been going, they've earned it. They're working so hard."

We've all been working hard. Getting the factory up and running again after the safety violation fiasco was no easy task, but in the past eight months, the plant has completely turned around.

After the big meeting at Roland Enterprises, Barrett and I went back to his apartment in Chicago with every intention of spending the whole night hashing out a plan for company restructuring. Admittedly, we were up all night doing anything but working, but that Monday morning, we rolled out a new plan for the factory.

More weekly meetings with my staff, more checks and balances, and more direct involvement on my part instead of spending nine-to-five inside of my office. Mark dropped all charges against the plant with the understanding that he'd have more direct involvement in the plant's design and safety, a role which I granted him immediately. The biggest difficulty was getting the factory up to working conditions again, but Barrett was generous enough to lend the factory the money for renovations.

I hesitated to take it until he reminded me he had a hand in shutting us down in the first place. Once we were back up and running, it hardly took any time before the factory hit its profit goal and I was able to pay back Barrett in full. Not that he was hurting for the money. Barrett Wilson and Associates took off the second he opened the doors of his practice. I guess small towns need sage legal advice too.

The four of us settle in at the picnic table with our plates, Barrett and me on one bench, Nick and Dana on the other.

"Looks great," I say, sizing up my plate.

"Not as great as you." Barrett places his hand on my thigh, and leans over and kisses me softly on the cheek, which Nick then mirrors with Dana. She giggles, tucking her hair behind her ear.

"I know I've said it again and again, but you two are beyond cute together," I say, which makes Dana giggles even more. Nick wraps his arm around her waist and scooches a little closer to her on the picnic bench.

"And to think if I didn't bail on you guys to go on a date with her, there may not be a Mr. and Mrs."

I roll my eyes toward my hubby, who is smirking into his burger. Nick loves retelling this story, claiming that it proves that he is the reason Barrett and I got together.

Mom tries to take credit for setting us up, too, arguing that she's the one who gave Barrett my number, but Dad says it was his doing since it was his retirement party. We stay quiet about it, letting them bicker and think whatever they want. Better not to tell them that it all started in our upstairs shower when I saw all of Barrett's...great qualities staring me in the face. And if I wanted to really analyze the hows and whys of our relationship, it really started decades ago when a girl fell in love with her brother's best friend.

Barrett turns toward me then, seemingly thinking the same thing, and places a soft kiss on my lips. "I love you, Ava."

"Loved you first."

Up Next

Birthday Sex by Kendall Ryan

Last night was the most embarrassing night of my life.

I was THAT girl.

You know, the highly intoxicated chick celebrating her thirtieth with her two best friends—the ones who are happily married. And the more I drank, the more I wanted to do something reckless to celebrate.

By reckless, I meant the sexy and alluring man dressed in a business suit standing near the bar. You know his type--tall, dark, handsome, and most of all, highly fuckable. I was sure he was out of my league, but I'd had just enough alcohol that things like that no longer seemed to matter. I'm not fat, mind you, but you can tell I like French fries, so there's that.

He took me home and I enjoyed the hottest birthday sex of my life, well until it came to a screeching, and rather unwelcome halt.

There's nothing quite like being interrupted mid-ride with a little voice asking:

"What are you doing to my daddy?"

Just kill me now…….. or so I thought.

Come to find out the man I rode like a bull at the rodeo is my new landlord.

Acknowledgments

A huge thank you to my entire dream team. Danielle Sanchez and Alyssa Garcia at Inkslinger PR, you rock my world. To Becca Mysoor at Evident Ink, dear God, woman, I can't believe you pulled an all-nighter with this book. I mean, you were smelling colors by the end, but it was worth it, right? A bear hug is in order for Elaine York. I truly love working with you. You make it so easy.

A massive thank you to Angela Marshall Smith, thank you for your guidance as I was crafting this story. Each of your read-throughs helped give it more heart, and for that I'm truly thankful. Thank you to Stephanie at Uplifting Designs for all the flexibility you were gracious enough to have during my crazy writing and editing schedule. Thank you to Virginia Tesi Carey for your eagle-eye editing, yet again. I am so grateful.

To Ava Erickson who is a consummate professional in all things, I seriously want to be you when I grow up. You make producing audiobooks look so effortless, and I'm in love with the way you, and Jacob Morgan bring my stories to life in that medium.

A huge bear hug to all of the book bloggers and readers for your excitement about Barrett and Ava's story. I am so appreciative of each and every review you left. A big thanks to Flavia and the amazing team at BookCase Literary. I'm thrilled to be on this journey and having you by my side makes it so much better.

I'm blessed to have so many amazing people in my life rooting me on, especially my sweet husband. Finally, I'm so incredibly blessed to have YOU as a reader. Thank you!

About the Author

A *New York Times*, *Wall Street Journal*, and *USA TODAY* bestselling author of more than two dozen titles, Kendall Ryan has sold over two million books, and her books have been translated into several languages in countries around the world. Her books have also appeared on the *New York Times* and *USA TODAY* bestseller list more than three dozen times. Kendall has been featured in publications such as *USA TODAY*, *Newsweek*, and *In Touch Magazine*. She lives in Texas with her husband and two sons.

Other Books by Kendall Ryan

Unravel Me

Make Me Yours

When I Break Series

Filthy Beautiful Lies Series

The Gentleman Mentor

Sinfully Mine

Bait & Switch

Slow & Steady

The Room Mate

Hard to Love

Resisting Her

Screwed

Dirty Little Secret

Dirty Little Promise

CPSIA information can be obtained
at www.ICGtesting.com
Printed in the USA
LVHW02s2256040918
589182LV00001B/166/P